A
TOR
DOUBLE

ACTION
WESTERN

W9-AWJ-816

Look for Tor Double Action Westerns from these authors

MAX BRAND
ZANE GREY
LEWIS B. PATTEN
WAYNE D. OVERHOLSER
CLAY FISHER
FRANK BONHAM
OWEN WISTER
STEVE FRAZEE*
HARRY SINCLAIR DRAGO*
JOHN PRESCOTT*
WILL HENRY*

*coming soon

Max Brand

CHIP CHAMPIONS
A LADY

FORGOTTEN TREASURE

TOR®

A TOM DOHERTY ASSOCIATES BOOK
NEW YORK

CHIP CHAMPIONS A LADY

Copyright 1931 by Street & Smith Publications, Inc.; copyright renewed 1959 by Dorothy Faust. First appeared in *Western Story Magazine*.

FORGOTTEN TREASURE

Copyright 1927 by Street & Smith Publications, Inc.; copyright renewed 1955 by Dorothy Faust. First appeared in *Western Story Magazine* as by ''George Owen Baxter.''

Compilation copyright © 1990 by Tor Books.

A Tor Book
Published by Tom Doherty Associates, Inc.
49 West 24th Street
New York, N.Y. 10010

Cover art by Ballestar

ISBN: 0-812-50538-7

First edition: September 1990

Printed in the United States of America

0 9 8 7 6 5 4 3 2 1

CHIP CHAMPIONS A LADY

• 1 •

Young Mrs. Newbold stood on the back porch of the new ranch house and sang out, "Chip! Oh, Chip!" I was mending a bridle in the shade of the bunkhouse, and Chip was beside me, whittling transparent shavings off a stick with a knife big enough to reach the heart of a bull and sharp enough to shave a three days' beard. He canted his head and scowled, when he heard the musical voice of the girl.

"Aw, leave me be!" he muttered under his breath.

"Chip!" called Marian Newbold. "Oh, Chip—dar-ling!"

"Darling?" said Chip under his breath. "Dang!"

He looked guiltily askance at me, reddening somewhat.

"You better sing out, Chip," I advised, "or else she'll be telling the whole valley that you're a darling—to her, anyway."

His freckled nose wrinkled at me. His wicked blue eyes gleamed.

"Doggone me if I ain't stood about enough of this!" he muttered.

But he stood up, rather in haste, and stepped out into the sunlight, where he could be seen. There he took off his man-sized sombrero—padded about the rim to fit his head—and waved it at her.

The sun flamed in his hair. Shooting fires seemed to crown him wildly.

"Hello, Marian," he called.

"Oh, Chip," says she, throwing out a hand toward him, and cocking her head with her smile. "I've got good news for you! Come here!"

Chip hesitated. He drew himself up to the full altitude and pride of sixteen winters—because there was not much of summer in that flinty young nature.

"Whatcha want?" demanded Chip, parleying for time.

"I want you, dear," says Marian Newbold, and she came down the steps and then down the path toward him, as lovely a thing as you'd want to see, all grace and consciousness. Chip made about three steps to meet her.

But she was not proud. She never was proud, with Chip. She went all the rest of the way and laid her slim hands on his shoulders.

"Dear Chip," says she, "everything is settled."

"About what?" asked Chip.

"About your school, of course. I've just had word from your Uncle Newbold—"

"He ain't any uncle of mine," declared Chip.

"By affection he is, Chip," said she.

Chip grunted.

"I dunno about that affection business," he answered. "You know, it's all right, but it don't make uncles. What's he gone and decided about me?"

"He's found the very place for you," runs on the girl, "where you'll continue to have the splendid outdoor life that you love so much, and horses to ride, and swimming, and tennis—"

"Tennis, eh?" says Chip, with a shrug.

"You don't have to play tennis, though," said Marian Newbold. "You don't have to do a single thing except try to please your Aunt Marian for one little, single term, Chip. I certainly can call myself your aunt, can't I, Chip, darling?"

He looked at her and sighed.

"Yeah," said he. "I guess you can call yourself anything you want to, Marian. But this here school business is—"

"It's the most wonderful place you ever heard of," said she. "And there are big woods, and running creeks, and a fine natural lake—"

"What would an unnacheral lake be like, Marian?" says Chip. "But go on."

"And I have the most charming letter from the matron, Chip. I want you to read it. I know that she's a dear. And you'd like her instantly, and she'd make you feel perfectly at home!"

"Yeah?" doubted Chip. "You know, Marian, it's a terrible lot of money to spend on school when you get lakes and rivers and everything throwed in and—and—"

"Oh, when you're grown up and rich, you'll pay back every penny of it," said Marian Newbold. "That's all decided. In the meantime, we're only lending a little and trying to help out."

"It's too much," says Chip. "I couldn't take it and—"

"Chip," says she, "you will go, to please your Aunt Marian who loves you?"

"Look here, Marian—" he began arguing.

"You know I love you, don't you, Chip?" says she.

"Yeah, sure, but you know—" he begins again.

"And you won't do one thing for me? One single small thing?" says she. "You really don't care a snap for me, Chip. I'm not asking much. I'm only asking you for one little promise. It won't be more than three months! And you'll have horses, and dogs, too. Everything will be the way you want it. Say 'yes,' Chip, please!"

With this, she kisses him, and Chip winces and blinks.

"Give me a little chance to think it over, Marian," says he. "Say, by tomorrow—"

"No, by tonight, by tonight!" says she.

She bends her head toward him again, with her pretty lips pursed.

"Yeah. All right, all right!" says Chip, wincing. "I'll tell you by tonight all right. Thanks, Marian!"

"Dear old Chip," says she, and gives him a bear hug.

She went off up the path to the house, singing, literally floating along.

And Chip came back to me very red indeed, wiping his mouth with the back of his hand, hard, and half avoiding my eyes, and half daring me to laugh at him.

"It's all right, Chip," said I. "Better men than you have been coaxed by a pretty girl."

He sat down, panting. He actually shuddered a little.

"The kind of trouble that they make for a man," said Chip, "it's a terrible thing just to think about it. She was gunna kiss me again, by Jiminy!"

He started at his whittling again, but he was so moved that he slashed the stick right in two at the next cut.

"Where you been this last trip?" I asked him, partly to start a new subject, and partly because I was genuinely interested.

"Oh, just around," he answered me.

"You've been with Waters. I suppose?" said I.

"Waters?" he answered vaguely, as though the name of the outlaw, his dearest friend, were one that he barely recognized. "It's a funny thing, Joe," said he, "how much people talk about Waters."

"Yeah, it's a funny thing," I admitted. "Poor Waters, he hasn't done a thing in the last six months except to stick up a couple of stages and shoot up the sheriff of Inyo County. Aside from that, he's hardly stirred. But you know how it is, Chip. People have to talk about something. And when there's no war, or nothing, going on, Waters is about the next best thing."

The boy grinned at me. He had an odd, flashing smile that was apt to twist only one side of his face a bit, as though only half of his mind was amused.

"They got nothin' on him," he averred. "They got nothin' on him about the stages, for one thing."

"I thought they identified him through some stuff that he pawned in El Paso?" I suggested.

"Him? He didn't steal that stuff," said the boy. "He just had bought it, and got tired of it."

"Yeah," said I. "I could imagine that after he'd bought a pearl necklace to wear around his pretty white neck he might get tired of it pretty quick."

Chip drove his knife into the ground with an angry jab.

"Anyway," he argued, feebly but sternly, "he didn't have nothing to do with the stickups."

"Nor the sheriff either, I suppose," said I.

"Of course he didn't," said Chip, vainly trying to meet my eye. "Besides, what's there wrong about a free fight? And a fair fight?"

"Aw, not a thing," said I. "Waters is all right."

"He's a friend of yours, Joe," said Chip, rather mournfully. "There's nothing that he wouldn't do for you, since that jailbreak—"

I jerked my head over both shoulders. There was no one near.

"Lay off of that, Chip," I warned him.

"Anyway, he's a friend of yours, for life. He'd never do you no harm, Joe. He'd come a thousand miles to help you out!"

"That's fine of him," said I.

He sighed. It appeared that something was on his mind and that he could not find a handle for it.

"Speakin' about women—" he began again.

As he paused, I helped him out.

"Have you found one that you take to, Chip?"

He did not smile, simply because he failed to see the humor in this, or the possibilities of humor. He was a little blind in that direction only—he never could look upon himself as other than a grown man, with all of a man's interests.

"Me?" he said with some haste. "No, I ain't built that way. I never seem to have no time to waste. Women—they make me—"

He stopped short. I was amazed by this show of tact.

"Go right on, Chip," said I. For I had heard him berate the entire female sex at great length, a good many times before this.

"Aw, they're fine," said Chip slowly. "I suppose that nobody's what he had oughta be until he's got himself married. No man is what a man oughta be, until he's gone an' got himself a danged smirkin', grinnin'—I didn't mean that either.''

He was all in a shiver. Suddenly he said, "Look at here, Joe.''

"Well, Chip?'' said I.

"What about yourself?'' he asked.

"What about what?''

"About yourself,'' he repeated. "What sort of a girl would you step out and marry, one of these days?''

I turned and looked hard at him. The drift of his thought was beyond me, but that was not surprising, for Chip's drift of thoughts generally was beyond me, anyway.

• 2 •

Aᴡᴀʏ ᴘᴀsᴛ Cʜɪᴘ, I ʟᴏᴏᴋᴇᴅ ᴀᴄʀᴏss ᴛʜᴇ sʜɪᴍᴍᴇʀ ᴏꜰ ᴛʜᴇ heat waves as they danced on the ridges, and across the hollows, too, and out to where a buzzard was circling. Somehow, it was like looking half across the world, or clear through the heart of something, I can't say what.

My fingers kept fumbling at the bridle that I was working on.

"Well," insisted Chip, "d'you see her face pretty clear, now?"

"Whose face?" said I.

"Her face—the girl's face—the one you wanta marry!" said Chip.

It wouldn't have done to let a man talk to me like that, but from Chip it was easy to take almost anything. So I laughed at him.

"You've got woman on the mind today, old son," said I.

He broke out in a regular snarl.

"Who could help havin' 'em on the mind?" he demanded. "Who could help wantin' to herd 'em all onto an island and then sink the island, and sink it deep, and wait till the last bubbles come up, and then go home and know that the best day's work in the world is done!"

"You know, Chip," said I, "the race would die out after that. You've got to have women in order to have men."

"Yeah, I know," said Chip. "But let the old race die, then. What's the use of having the race go on, if it's gunna be pestered and bothered all the time? There's no use. Let the old cat die, if it's gotta. It's better to let it die than to keep it dizzy, always. The way men are now, about women. There's women everywhere and they're behin' everything. If you hear a gun go off, it's because of a woman. If you hear a door slam, it's because of a woman. There's woman in everything, and I'm pretty sick of 'em—danged sick of 'em!"

I sighed as I watched Chip. It was true. I had often felt it before, when in talk with him. He was free. There were no trammels upon him. There was not even the binding grace of any great affection, except his blind and noble devotion to Waters, the outlaw. So Chip could stand, as it were, upon an eminence, from which he commanded a spreading view of the follies of man.

And yet, in only a year or two, the height would be cut from beneath his feet, and he would roll in the dust among the rest of us poor mortals.

"Go on," said Chip. "You're true-blue, Joe. You wouldn't dodge. You tell me the truth—that there's some girl that you got your heart pretty set on."

"No," said I.

"Is that straight?"

"You bet it's straight just now," said I.

"You mean that you been in an' out a lot of times?" asked Chip.

"In and out of what?" said I.

"Love," said Chip, making a face as he used the word.

"Oh, sure," said I. "I been in and out a lot of times."

"Like with what?" asked Chip.

"What are you driving at, Chip?" said I.

"Aw, g'wan and tell me, Joe," he urged.

I considered him again. I had a feeling that he was thus curious for no very good or kindly reason. Nevertheless, it was always easy to talk to Chip. What one said to him was placed in a sealed book which would be opened to no other eyes.

"You want me to tell you about the girls that I've been dizzy about. Is that it?" I asked. "You wanta laugh at me, Chip?"

He reached out a hand in a sudden gesture, as though to reassure me, almost as though to protect me—he a boy of sixteen and I a grown man.

"No, I wouldn't laugh at you, Joe," said he. "But g'wan and tell me, will you?"

"Well, it's like this," said I. "The first time I was a kid just a jump older than you, and it was a girl that wore a broad blue ribbon in her hair, and she was always smiling. She had so many teeth that she had to."

"I don't mean calf love," said Chip, irritated.

"Every love affair is calf love, I suppose," said I. "The second was a waitress with a good-natured way. I'd ridden into a strange town on a strange range, and she sort of made me at home. She had a motherly way about her. But the look of her hands finally finished me. There was always a little grease about 'em, you know."

"Yeah. Don't I know!" said Chip, disgusted.

"Then I got up in the world and got dizzy about a school-teacher who knew how to look at you sideways and make your heart jump—"

"Like a broncho, side-jumping, maybe?" asked Chip, listening with a frown of interest.

"Something like that," said I. "The next was a tall brunette who wore her clothes pretty tight to show off her figure. But the boys were always crowding around her, and when I saw that I'd never be more than one in a crowd, I swallowed my heartache and rode away."

Chip stifled a yawn. Yet his interest returned, almost fiercely. And he said, "That's four. Go on, Joe."

"I met a nice Swede girl from Indianapolis," said I. "We went out riding together, and it was a spring evening, and the mist in the hollow was in the blue of her eyes. And she looked sort of dewy and fresh—"

"All right," said Chip, cutting in to avoid the details. "What come next?"

"There was a mighty good-natured girl down on the Staked Plains," said I, "that was as brown as you ever saw, and a good, hearty laugh, down in her throat like the laugh of a man—"

"Did you stick to her?" asked Chip.

"To her?" said I. "She went off and married a drummer. Fellow who sold farming implements, you know. That was all right. I mourned a good deal about her till I met a Denver girl with a thin back but a stylish way and—"

"Aw, say," broke in the boy, "to cut it all short, did you ever fall in love with a girl at first sight?"

"No," said I. "That's a lot of boloney—that falling in love at first sight. Don't you believe in that, Chip. It's the bunk."

"Boloney, is it?" said Chip. "Well, I've seen it happen, and that's all I gotta say."

I wondered more than ever what he was driving at.

He went on, "What about a Mexican girl? Ever fall in love with a Mexican girl, Joe?"

"No," said I. "I don't want any Maria Tortilla for mine."

He nodded at me, like an old man at a child.

"You think of something brown on the skin and burnt in the eyes," he suggested. "But what I mean is first-class, genuine Castile."

"That's a good soap," said I. "Kind of yellowish, though, and it don't float."

"Yeah?" said the boy.

He looked coldly on me. I felt that he was about to deliver me a blow, and I was distinctly right. I was about to have a dagger plunged into my vitals.

"Go on, Chip," said I. "You tell me about this brand of soap that you're peddling."

"That's what I'm gunna do," said he. "I'm gunna sell you a package," he even declared.

I laughed a little, but uneasily. "Go on, then," said I.

"There ain't far to go," said Chip. "Here you are."

And with that, he took out of his inside coat pocket a

leather case, and from the case he removed a flat packet wrapped in softest chamois, and under the chamois there was a wrapping of finest silk, and within the silk, hulled like a body of flesh and spirit, there was a square of ivory, and on the ivory was painted the portrait of a girl who looked at me, by thunder, with such eyes that I swore she knew me, and knew that I was looking back, and was glad that I looked.

Now, I never knew enough about painting to tell whether that work was good or bad, or whether it was too rosy and olive, too dreamy in the eyes, too sweet and smiling about the mouth; and, I suppose that the colors were crude and the work bad. But to me, the thing was living. I took out a handkerchief and mopped my forehead.

"All right," said Chip.

I looked up at him and his disdainful face.

"You limb, you," said I. "You've done this on purpose. You've gone and knocked the wind out of me."

He shrugged. "Go on and ask your questions," he said, resigned. "Only, you answer me one, first."

"I'll answer anything, Chip," said I, staring down into the eyes of the miniature.

"You tell me straight, a second time: There ain't such a thing as love at first sight?"

I couldn't even smile. I only choked. Then I said, "You're right, Chip. You're right about everything, even love at first sight. Though how you learned of that I don't know."

"I wished I'd died before I did," said Chip grimly. "Go on, now, and ask me if she really does look like that."

"You mean that this ain't some old master?" said I. "You mean that this here girl is in the flesh, somewhere?"

"Yeah, that's what I mean," said he. I took the ivory in both hands.

"Give it back to me," said he.

"Go to the dickens, Chip, old partner," said I. "This here is never gunna leave my hands until I've seen her."

"Aw, you can see her, all right," said Chip.

"Boy," said I, "can you lead me to her?"

"What else did I come all the way up here for except for that?" demanded Chip.

"And why should you?" said I.

"Because the poor girl's in trouble."

My head spun. "She looks like this, Chip?" said I.

"Lemme see," said he, critically examining the portrait. "Yeah, her eyes is like that, but when she smiles, it's like lightin' a lamp. You never seen the like. You can see to read by when she's around; there ain't no night too dark."

"And you're so fond of her that you came all the way to get me to help her out of this trouble?" said I.

"That's it," said Chip. "She needs help, and that's why I'm here."

He looked me straight in the eye, and his brow was as smooth and untroubled as marble, and his glance was as open, as pure, and as straight as the blue look of a mountain lake.

So I knew that Chip was lying with all the might of his mighty heart.

• 3 •

I STUDIED CHIP FOR A TIME. I KNEW THAT WE WERE SUCH good friends, and such old ones, that he was not apt to intend any harm for me. And yet I could not but feel that his yarn was very odd, and that it might be hiding all sorts of reefs and shoals for my navigation.

"What's the trouble that she's in?" I asked.

Chip sighed.

"Ay," he said. 'That's the way of it! I knew that sooner or later you'd ask me that question; but you see, Joe, it's a thing that you wouldn't believe, if I was to tell you. And the only way that you could possibly think it true would be to hear it right from the lips of Doloritas Ruan."

"Is that her name?"

"Yeah, that's her name."

At least, he was not lying about that. I turned the name on my tongue, and though I turned it in silence, I could hear a golden voice naming at my ear, over and over, "Maria de los Dolores," and all its musical variations—"Doloritas," "Dolorcitas," "Lola," "Lolita." And with all of them, "Ruan" went very well at the end.

So I looked down at the miniature again, and the black magic spread through my veins. I cannot tell how it was that even then I felt that there was danger and all manner of trouble wrapped up in this thing. But know it I did. Some extra sense was working in me—that and the knowledge that Chip was lying about something, or holding back, or saying too much.

"Chip," I said, "do you think I'll go with you to help this Maria de los Dolores? I don't care what her sorrows are, unless I know them!"

Chip shrugged. "Oh, you'll come, all right," said he. And he grinned at me, and suddenly I knew that he was right.

"Tell me this," said I. "Is she married?"

He thought for a long moment, and then he shook his head.

"I oughtn't to talk about her," said he. "That's a thing that I mustn't do!"

"You ought to give me a chance at the truth," said I. "You've got to tell me something—that much, at least. Is she married?"

"No," he finally indulged me. "She's not married. I'm telling you that on the promise that you won't badger me with a lot of problems and questions all the way south."

"To where she is?" said I. "D'you think, Chip, that I'll fly off and leave my job and go away with you on a wild-goose chase like this?"

He looked me flat in the eye. He had the nerve of a brass monkey.

"You'll just about do that," he declared. "You know that this old strawboss job will be waiting for you whenever you wanta come back and take it up again. You don't care much about it, anyway. Nobody enjoys workin' much under old Newbold. I know that. Because I've worked for him myself!"

I laughed a little, thinking of those hay-press days when Chip had badgered us all so thoroughly and driven us like a gadfly. A gadfly he was, stinging men on to strange performances. Well, I was terribly uneasy, but every now and again I looked down to the ivory, and the beauty and the strangeness of that face went through me with a tingling shock of sweetness. Yes, that lad was right.

"How far is it?" I snapped at him.

"Ten days' riding," said he.

"Not any train riding?"

"No. Hosses. And mules, maybe."

"Mountain work, then?"

"I've said enough," said Chip. "I told you that I wouldn't answer no more questions."

"You've gotta answer one, though," said I. "Here you've come like a homing pigeon ten days north to find me. Why did you come all this ways? Why did you come specially to me?"

He shook his head.

"You won't tell me?" I insisted.

He shook his head again, and set his teeth, and yet I could see some sort of an answer glimmering in his eyes.

"You've got to tell me, Chip," said I.

At last he burst out, "I will tell you, Joe, if you'll promise me that it's the last question."

I took a quick, deep breath. I knew that I was a fool. I've already said that I felt danger fairly humming in this situation. But still I was tempted, and all the sweet voices of romance were making music in my brain.

"Well, Chip," said I, "I'll make that promise—though I still won't promise to go. I won't ask you another question if you'll tell me why you really picked me out from the whole world to do the job."

"Because," he said with the utmost solemnity, "there ain't another man in the world that could do it!"

There might have been a good deal of question about his other remarks before this one, but there was no doubt at all about the ringing sincerity in his voice now.

"And you know, Joe," he continued, leaning toward me, "that I wouldn't want you to risk your life, neither, if it wasn't a job worthwhile."

"Risk my life?" said I, with sudden pressure choking me. "Risk my life?" said I, and the hair stirred and prickled upon my skull, and against my very brainpan.

"Ay, risk your life," said Chip huskily. "You're my old partner, Joe, ain't you?"

"Ay," said I. "We're partners, Chip. But what's this idea about life and death—" I made a feeble attempt at a laugh.

But Chip shook his head mournfully.

"You'd have about one chance in three of pulling through," he said. "That's about all the chance that you'd have, old partner. But it's the kind of a grand game that I know you'd really like to play."

He was getting fired up.

"You keep your Irish blood tamed down, will you?" said I. "You know me, Chip. Or you ought to. There's no Irish in me. There's nothing in me that hankers after grandeur and adventures. I'm willing to sit back on my haunches and wait for my time to marry some hashslinger or—"

My voice petered out. I was looking down at the picture of Doloritas, and the sight of it stopped me at once.

"You're gunna do a great thing," said the boy to me. "You're gunna do a thing that'll make you happy for life, and pretty famous, and you'll have Doloritas, besides. Why, old son, the smile that she'll give you when you arrive will make your ten days of riding seem just like one afternoon. And now I've gotta be sloping. Are you the man that's riding south with me, Joe?"

"Hold on, hold on!" I exclaimed. "You can't leave. You gotta see Marian Newbold again."

"I wouldn't see her again," said the boy, "for a thousand dollars a minute. You can say good-by to her for me, will you?"

"And get blamed for your going?" said I.

"That's all right," said he. "They won't hold no grudges against the two of us."

I knew he was right, and yet I was ashamed to go in and face Marian. She could chill her manner and her words on the warmest sort of a day, and I didn't want to be frosted all over.

However, I saw that he was stubborn. He was afraid of another affectionate demonstration, I suppose. So I went into

the house and spoke to Marion. She gave me one of her
kindest smiles. She was always kind to me, but I knew that
she wasn't interested. There was only one man in the world.
That was Newbold. There was only one outside person—until
her own kids should begin to arrive—and that was Chip.

"Marian," said I, "Chip's decided not to go to school."

"What?" she cried. "Chip gone?"

She ran to the window. I followed after. And through the
window we could see a mule with a bald and mangy rump
going down the southern valley trail, and there was a small
rider in the saddle, a rider slewed well around to the side—
the very manner of Chip in the saddle.

"Oh, Chip, oh Chip!" said Marian, and wrings her hands.
"You'll never give yourself a chance to be what you could
be!"

"Listen, Marian," said I. "What kind of a school could
he go to? What kind of other boys could he find there that
would stand the wear and tear of being shaken around inside
of any set of walls with that cast-iron bombshell, that Chip?
What sort of a school would stand that wear and tear? Why,
away out here in the West, where they talk about the open
spaces, things are sort of crowded with one Chip. There isn't
even room on your ranch for him. You know how things go
when he's around here?"

She sighed. "I love him!" said she logically.

"Sure you do," said I. "You women always love a trou-
blemaker. And that's where he's bound now—to find trouble.
And I'm going along after him!"

She caught her breath and turned around sharp on me. She
put her hand on my arm and peered into my face, in a rather
frightened way.

"Do you mean it, Joe?" said she.

"Yeah," said I. "I mean it, all right. I'm starting now. I
don't like to step out of the job like this. But you know how
it is."

"I don't know how it is," said she.

"You will, if you take another think. The only reason that

the chief wants me around here is not that I'm an extra good puncher, but because he feels that he's my friend.''

''And he is your friend,'' said she.

''Yeah, but he doesn't need me. He's able to do his own bossing of his men, goodness knows. So I'm sliding out from under. I'm following Chip.''

''Where?'' said she.

''I don't know. Just south,'' said I.

She sighed again. There was a real pity in her eyes.

''Dear old Joe,'' says she. ''Do you think it's wise to ride blindly on the sort of trail that Chip, of all people, is likely to follow?''

It angered me a little, I admit, the way she sort of talked down to me.

''I'm not the toughest hombre in the territory,'' said I. ''But still, I've stood the wear and tear so far. I've worked with the chief long enough to callous up some of the tender spots. I'll take my chances with Chip on the trail.''

''Oh, Joe—'' she began.

''Well, what?'' said I.

But then I saw that there were tears in her eyes, and a tremor in her lips, so I backed out and said good-by and left at once.

· 4 ·

When I rolled my pack and strapped it on the back of the roan, I was still feeling a little blue. It's all very well to have a woman treat one in almost any way, except one. A man will stand anything from a girl with a pretty face—anything except pity. And I had last seen Marian Wray Newbold with her eyes filled with tears of pity as she looked at me.

Why?

She didn't know what danger might be on this trail, though she might guess that Chip did not ordinarily ride for the mere fun of seeing landscape. But why pity me so heartily?

You see, I could ride about as well as the next man, I could handle a rope, do my job riding the range, and shoot enough game to keep me in fresh meat if I had an hour a day for the hunting. I was man-sized, reasonably well set up, and on the whole I could pass in most crowds. The sag of my broken nose didn't make me beautiful, to be sure; but it wasn't on account of my looks that Marian Newbold had been pitying me.

Well. I knew why, too.

It was because I was just ordinary Western iron, and whatever job the kid was steering for was apt to require steel tools. Iron is a good, tough metal, too. And you can put a reasonable edge on it. But steel will cut it through like butter, almost.

Newbold—there was a fellow of steel. You could put an edge on him, and he wouldn't grow dull through a lifetime of pounding. And "White" Waters, whom Chip worshiped so—there was another fellow all steel—a finer temper, even, than Newbold, I suspected, though Newbold worked inside of the law and the other worked outside it. But I was not that sort of stuff. I was only iron. I could cut wood, so to speak, but I couldn't cut rock.

Well, I could shoot fairly well with a revolver or a rifle. And I think I had average nerve. But the difference between me and a Newbold or a Waters was—simply that between iron and steel.

I reflected on this as I rode down the trail after the boy. And I began to wonder more and more. Chip knew my failings. He knew that I was no more than an average man. And when he had a hero like Waters at his beck and call, why should he have ridden for ten days to get hold of me?

Perhaps Waters was down. Perhaps he'd been hurt in some recent escapade. At any rate, here I was, committed to the trail with a piece of painted ivory for my commission, and my tongue chained by the foolish promise which I had made to the boy.

It hurt me a good deal. It hurt me to think that I was such a fool. And it hurt me to know that every one could see through to my weaknesses as if they were looking through a glass window into my heart. Marian, among the rest. It's not so bad to be looked down upon by men, big and important men. But it's hard to have the very women see one's weaknesses.

I was beginning to scowl and put on a fighting face, when I turned a corner of the trail and there I found that Chip was waiting for me. He said by way of greeting, "Does that roan take to the mountain trails pretty well?"

"That roan," said I, "will walk wherever a mountain goat walks."

"Mountain goats," said the kid, "never were seen in the country where we're going."

"No?" said I.

I grinned at the freckled face of Chip. It was good to be out there on the trail with him again, no matter what was ahead of us. No matter what else he did, he made me forget about women, confound them!

"No," repeated Chip, shaking his head seriously. "Where we're going the goats get dizzy, and even the flies make it a step at a time, and the bees go trembling along the edge of nothin' at all."

"Above timberline, is it?" said I.

"Above timberline?" said he.

Then he laughed.

"Why, old partner," said Chip, "them that have climbed up to where we're going forget that there ever was such a thing as a tree in this little old world of ours!"

It was good, as I said before, to hear Chip stretching things again, but just the same it was not exactly reassuring.

And so we went along the trail, and to cut a long story short, we climbed two ranges, and crossed two valleys, and we got into the wildest heart of the Mogollons.

I hear people rave and rage about great and famous mountains, and Alps, and such things, but the Mogollans are good enough for me. They're high enough to fall off and crack your sconce, and they're high enough to catch the rain clouds and squeeze the water out of them to the last drop. I've seen storms good enough for Antarctica or the North Pole right there among the Mogollons, and cliffs that jump a man's mind into the heart of the sky, or drop it down the bottom of the well to the hot place.

And there's something wild about the Mogollans. They haven't been tramped over and camped over as much as other mountains. They're like a Western mustang, just full of humps, and bumps, and meannesses, and twists, and angles, and shakes. They're bad enough to fill a book. Not even a dude ranch can flourish out there in the Mogollons. But I've known people who loved those mountains because of their wildness. And I'm one of the people that I talk about.

There are other things than mountains and mountain forms to be seen down yonder. There are mining towns, here and there, and where the grass is good enough, you'll find regular cattle ranches; and hither and yon will always be a bright bit of old Mexico dropped down into a sheltered corner, all white and red, like a Sunday washing of table linen and red flannels!

There's a peculiarity about the Mexicans that most people don't notice, and that's the ease with which they establish their boundary lines.

The Rio Grande is a mighty small stream. And on the north side of it there's all the fuss, and the bother, and the stamping and the dusting about the greatest nation on earth; that's enough to establish the northern side of the boundary wall.

But on the south side of the stream, there's only a sleepy, good-humored and lazy lot of soft voices, and dark eyes, and dusty streets, and the wind goes one way and the river goes another, and nobody gives a darn.

But that southern boundary is as strongly marked as the northern one. You can see, and feel, and smell Mexico when you're halfway across the international bridge.

Up there in the New Mexico mountains it's the same way. Where the Mexicans have formed their communities—and they've made plenty of them, of course!—one leaves the soil of the United States—the spirit of the Americans, at least— and passes instantly into another world, spiritual and physical.

So it came to us on this day which was to pass me out of my old world and into a new one.

We dropped over a miserable trail that zigzagged like a lightning scar down the face of cliff; and so we came into a white alkali flat where birds and beasts were whitish, too; and we went over this flat that shone and dazzled beneath us, casting up a fiery reflection so strong that it scorched us beneath the chin and under the eyes, until we came to a dry draw where the water must have run strongly in the rainy season. But now the bed was filled with the last evidences of the waterwork. The boulders and the strewings of smaller rocks lay just as the hands of the currents had last let them fall, and all was gleaming and bright under the sun.

There was a staggering bridge that crossed this draw, but it looked a little feeble to us, so we took our way down one bank, up the other, and so came out again into the continuation of the trail beyond. And there, immediately beside us, we saw the shrine of a saint—I don't know which one—with the boarding which had hooded it fallen away, and the wooden face of the image lifted in suffering to whatever weather might be.

I looked at this shrine with a good deal of curiosity. It was carved rather roughly, but it had great expression, and the fellow who did that work must have found a model of suffering in his own heart. Otherwise, he never could have cut so close to the quick.

With equal interest I looked at another thing. On the little platform just under the shrine there was lying a pair of old spurs, nailed in place, simply, by forcing the rowels into the wood. Those rowels were the big-fingered Mexican kind, and they had rusted almost to nothing, long ago. I wondered over them. A Mexican may treat his horse with contempt, but he usually treats his spurs with the utmost tenderness. And here these had been left to the work of the weather! Well, they were an offering, of course. And I could not help trying to surmise what man, hounded across country on a bitter chase, by the law, or else trekking slowly across the desert, in the moment of his necessity had vowed his very spurs to this little wayside saint if he could win through to safety.

It must have been so.

From this moment, the air and the atmosphere of the United States were altered, and in their place, we were riding through old Mexico with a vengeance.

As we got across the valley and into the first rise of the trail beyond, we got out of the gray region of the cactus, the agave, and the yucca to the belt of greasewood and sagebrush, with the heat still increasing, because the slant of the slope held us flat in place for the sun to beat against. And here we passed a broken house of adobe. All the upper walls were gone. Most of the bricks had dissolved with rain and wind, but some lay broken on the ground, and one could see the clumsy and familiar handmade care which had produced them. This hut had consisted of two rooms, for one could look in on the floor plan. And there had been no outhouses, apparently. It had stood there in the low-blowing smoke of the greasewood, an utter desolation. No white man could have chosen to build his home in such a place, far from good wood and water, far from good hunting, too, far from grasslands. But a Mexican will build wherever the impulse stirs in him, and only the saints can tell when and where the impulse will budge him.

This mouthful of emptiness made my brain ring like a rusty tin pan and I went on with the boy, shivering a little. Even Chip looked askance at that sorry bit of ruin, and twisted his mouth a little.

We passed over slopes spotted with cedar; we climbed to the region of pine and fir, and got into thin, pure air, two miles above the sea. Then we dived through a twisting gorge, half blocked by the remnants of an ancient Spanish fort. Why should there have been a fort here? That again only the Mexican mind could have answered! And so we came twisting down through the peaks and at last came out into the view of a little flat bottom valley, a Mexican valley of rocks, and pines, and grassland.

I SAY IT WAS A MEXICAN VALLEY BECAUSE PART OF THE grasslands were farmed, and the farms were not checked off in square fields but were worked in long strips, such as the peon loves to set out and till. And I could see men toiling in those fields and by their bent backs one could tell from the distance that they were not Americans. For Americans may bend in labor, but they don't seem to stay bent. In a hayfield, or even with a spade, your true American seems to be standing erect most of the time. But an Italian or a Mexican always appears to be bent over like a pin that never will be straightened for fear of breaking it.

Those fellows were peons. I could swear. And, besides, the Mexican atmosphere of which I speak, which had been thickening ever since we passed the shrine and the spurs, now rose in a steam, as it were, from this little, half-barren valley. The very shapes of the rocks were not American, it seemed to me, but were twisted and flattened and carved and chopped by nature, as nature generally is south of the Rio Grande. Even the pine trees which formed good plantations here and there were not American, if I dare say it. And right across from us, I saw, well up from the floor of the valley, crowning and overflowing the top of a hill, what seemed half house and half fort. Or, rather, it looked like a house that, on occasion, had had to play the part of a fort as well.

Its bastions ran down over the sides of the hill. It had a great, broad patio into which I could look. And I saw that half of the roof was fallen in. Little streams and trailers of greenery, glittering like running water beneath the sun ran down over the walls of this ancient house. And still they ran down, trickling and twisting beside the trail that ran from the dignified entrance gate to the level of the valley beneath.

Some inspiration came to me, and a chill along with it. I pointed toward the house.

"Doloritas lives yonder, Chip!" I exclaimed.

He gave me one of his quick side glances.

"Yes," said he. "How come—"

But he did not deign to finish his questions. Instead, he looked with mournful eyes across the valley. There was a certain hopelessness in his face that I never had seen there before.

"Yeah. Lolita lives there," he concluded. And he shook his head dismally.

"I thought you said that we were going to travel above timberline to get to the place?" I asked him, both relieved and disappointed. For now that we were near the goal, I rather wished that we still had other days of traveling before us.

"Well, we have been above timberline plenty since we started," said Chip. Then he added, "You don't think that this here is very high. But you'll see. It's been high enough to make me pretty dizzy. It's likely to make you dizzy, too! You wanta watch yourself, up here on these trails, Joe. Because a lot of people have missed their steps and taken a thousand-foot drop. That's a mighty lot of dropping to do all in one step, I'd say."

"Yes. I guess they thought so," said I, feebly amused.

"Well, there you are," said he. "That's the place that you're bound for."

"Why do you wave me on, Chip?" said I.

"Because that's where your trail lies, ain't it?" said he. He was irritated.

"Are you going to stay behind?" I asked, more and more alarmed.

"What should I wanta go in there for?" he asked me, as sharply and as unreasonably as before. "They'd only sink a knife into me between the shoulder blades, so's I wouldn't know the face of him that stuck me. No, no, Joe, old son. That's your job—the entering of the house!"

I felt the color draining out of my face. My skin felt puckered with cold fear.

"What sort of people are they, then, in yonder?" said I. "Is that a murder den?"

He started to shake his head and then, fixing his eyes steadily and coldly upon mine, he nodded several times, slowly.

"Yeah," he said, "there's been murders done in there." And he paused, as though sullenly waiting for me to refuse to enter such a place.

I bit my lip. I never wanted so badly to get away from the sight of any place as I wanted to get away from this one. But two things pushed me forward. One was the ten days of accumulated travel behind me, dammed up and pressing against me like gathered water power; and the other was the picture of Doloritas which was folded in its silken sheathing and lay nearest to my heart. Besides, there was my pride, whatever I had of that, telling me that I could not afford to shame myself before this boy. I sighed a little. I felt rather beaten.

"I thought that you were going through this thing with me, Chip," I told him, mournfully.

"Aw, Joe," said he, "buck up a little, won't you? What good would it be, I'm askin' you, for me to go along with you? The minute that they seen me, everything would be up, and they'd just slam us both."

"Why would everything be up?" I asked him. "What have you ever done to the people in that house?"

He groaned, impatient with himself for his last speech, as it appeared, and annoyed by my lack of resolution.

"I've done enough talking," said he, "and I've answered enough questions, and that's a fact."

"All right," said I.

But I found myself moistening my dry lips and still staring across at that house on the hill top, which seemed to be growing larger and larger every moment.

"I'd like to know what sort of people are inside of that house. That's all I'd like to ask you, Chip," I finally said to him.

He seemed to hesitate, doubting the wisdom of making an answer.

Then he replied: "I'll tell you. They're people just the opposite of everything they seem. That's about all I can tell you of 'em."

That was as little cheering and comforting as any answer I ever have received in my life!

"Chip," said I, "it's pretty hard lines. I'm not any hero, and it needs a hero to go up there into the house, I tell you. A hero compared with me, at least. But I'm going to try to drag myself along. Only—I expected that you would be with me!"

He held out his hand to meet the one I proffered. Then, as our grips closed, he gave my fingers a great squeeze.

"I'd like to be with you," said Chip. "But bein' a hero wouldn't help a man—not up there in that house!"

"What is that would help a man, then?" said I.

He rolled his eyes rather wildly.

"Luck!" he said at last. "Nothin' but luck!"

And he jerked his mule around and went riding back up the trail down which he had brought me.

It was a hard thing for me to sit there in the saddle and see the last of him. My heart was weakening all the time. And I stared after him until, at the last corner, he turned and gave me a wave of his hat, and he was still waving when the rock shut him away from my sight.

I turned, then, and looked again at the old house-fortress in its ruin. It stood up brightly in the mountain sunshine. Its rock wall glowed; its greenery flashed like running water;

and suddenly it seemed to me that the house, the valley, the trees, the rocks, the blue-headed mountains beyond, were all part of a picture which some hand had painted before, and here was I riding into the margin of a scene of the imagination.

This odd thought was so strong in me that it enthralled me completely. I looked down fixedly into the valley. It seemed to me that not a laborer had stirred from the moment I first saw them, and that they were not stirring now.

There was a horse and a high-wheeled cart in the near distance, off to the left, on a crookedly winding road. I stared at this cart until I saw it twist a little as it struck a rut.

Then I wakened from my daydream.

"Well," said I to myself, "shall I go on, or shall I hold back? I'll hold back, if I have my sense. I'll go on, if I'm a fool. And a fool is what I've always been!"

The horse began to walk forward of its own volition and instantly I accepted this as a token that I was meant to form a part and a portion of that picture which I saw before me.

And, as the roan went forward, I had a weird feeling, stronger than before, that I had ridden through the frame of the picture, and that now I was a part of it.

Or, to put it another way, that now I was something to be looked at, framed and hung on the wall, stared at by a casual, uninterested eye that might be bored, or indifferent, or, perhaps, cruelly malignant, and might choose, at just this point, to poke a finger through the canvas, or blur to nothingness this spot of the wet paint.

When I had got over some of this dreamy emotion—with the first sharp stumble of the horse—I began to use my eyes a little more carefully, and as I got down into the valley, I saw that it was a poor place. A good place for looking, you might say, but a poor place for soil. Elbow grease and fertilizer might raise some ragged crops of oats and corn down yonder, but the land was not meant to produce.

It was barren. It was as barren as the old oil paint on a canvas.

However, I could see the signs of life in actual movement,

as I got down into the floor of the valley. Dust I saw thinly curling up from the wheels of the distant cart, and then from a field almost as far away, I heard a wailing Mexican song.

Yes, the laborers were moving at their work, and my dream was beginning to come to life, with me in the center of it.

I headed straight across the flat breast of the plain toward the house on the hill. I crossed the darting face of the creek that ran through it, chiseling through the rocks so that I could measure the shallow scratchings of the surface soil, scant inches deep. Over the humpbacked little bridge I went, and saw my crooked image dim in the swift water beneath; and I passed from the hollow sound of the hoofbeats on the bridge to the quiet of the road beyond, and so wound up and up toward the gate of the house.

I could see, now, why there was greenery along the trail, because a runlet of water made a gutter on either side. Because of that spring this site must have been chosen for the building.

And I came up to the great, thick wall, and saw the gate made of ponderous beams and crossbars of time-whitened pine, sagging open. I looked about me. There was no bell to ring, nothing to knock on. It would have been, besides, like calling aloud to the dead centuries. So I rode on through and was up the slant and passing into the patio, when I heard a heavy, booming, crashing sound behind me.

I jerked about in the saddle, and saw that the gates had shut behind me, and still were quivering from the force with which they had been slammed together.

· 6 ·

I WANTED TO RUN BACK AND JUMP FROM THE SADDLE FOR the top of that gate and try to get out that way. I was fairly blind with the impulse to try it, but I kept the impulse locked back somewhere behind my teeth. The thing that had slammed those gates was watching me, of course, like a spider in its den.

I was the fool and the fly!

I decided that I had better show as little emotion as possible. This was a trap; I was inside it; and there was no use in jumping over a precipice just to please whatever bloated scoundrel was standing behind the scenes watching me.

A very odd thing, that. I mean, that from the instant that gate slammed I felt that whatever power controlled that house had the form of something swollen out of normal human shape. It was as clear in my mind as something already seen, and then more than half forgotten.

I went about my movements slowly and deliberately. I was shaking in my boots, but I dismounted, and threw the reins over the head of the roan, and that tough little brute amused itself picking at the grass which grew up through the cracks in the paving stones of the patio, and the crevices between them. There was no nerves in that mustang; that was the reason I had selected it for this mountain work.

And now I couldn't help remembering what Chip had said about heights and dizzy places. I was on one of them now. I was a mile above terra firma, it seemed.

I looked about that patio while I made a cigarette. Making a cigarette is the most soothing thing in the world, because it gives the hands something to do, and when the hands are safely occupied, for some reason or other, the brain has a better chance and the nerves will stop jumping.

There was not a soul in view from where I stood, and I seemed to see everything. The patio was apparently a big square, with a blank wall at the north, and an arcade running around the other three sides. A rough arcade of stones that had been quarried not for uniform size or color, but just to fit in haphazardly. It was ponderous work, and yet it was joined together with that sort of cunning which Indian masons always have shown. Those columns seemed to budge and stagger from side to side and in and out, and yet I knew perfectly well that this heavy masonry would outlast steel skyscrapers. Why had the roof fallen in, then, over a section of the house—as I had seen from the distance? No weight of time was apt to have crushed it; the force must have exploded from inside.

There was very little to see in the patio. There was the remains of a fountain in the very center, but it had been disused for so long that the bowl was all cracked, and the green scum that had dried around the sides of it had faded to white. The only thing that lived in that court was the dull green of the moss inside the northern wall. When I raised my head from the lighting of my smoke, I snapped the match suddenly and forcefully away.

For in front of me, leaning against one of the rude pillars of the arcade, I saw a Mexican standing, his feet crossed, his arms folded, a sneering smile on his face as he watched me.

He was just a round-faced peon of the lowest class, it seemed, but now he was looking me over from a height, as it were. He was complacent, as though he had felt the whip and expected me to feel it soon.

If you can guess the house from its servant, the Casa Ruan was a junk heap. This fellow wore a shapeless white cotton shirt, white cotton trousers cut off at the bulge of his brown calf, and a tattered straw hat. His feet were stuck into the ordinary huaraches, and for a weapon, he had stuck into his belt the machete which the Mexicans understand and love as the old French used to love rapiers.

He looked me over for a moment, while I drew down a deep breath of smoke in order to brace back my shoulders and recover a little from the shock of seeing him. Then he made a gesture to follow him, and walked through the shade and spotting sun beneath the arcade to the farther side of the patio.

I followed him, and went through an open arch into the southern garden of the house.

It was ten or twenty degrees warmer than the patio. Once it had been formed with care, the rock trenched, and the soil brought to the trenches. Now most of that soil had been washed or blown away, and there was only a ragged semblance of a garden, outlined in shrubs. The winding paths were half seen and half lost in the bracken. But yet this had been a garden, once, and a noble one. It needed no more than its view to still give it a certain dignity, for the eye looked out from it over the great, trembling void of the valley, with the mountains heaped up incredibly high beyond.

I gave these things something like a tenth of a second's observation. There was something else to take my attention. For there, stretched out in a sort of invalid's chair, taking the sun fearlessly, without a hat on his head, was the spider.

I mean, there lolled the controlling power of the house. One felt it by an instinct.

I would like to linger for a moment over the picture of him, partly because of what he was to do, and partly because I would like to speak of the various chills and electric currents that ran all at once, in a single pulse, through various crannies of my body, mind, and soul. Sensations of a mild fear, and interest, and loathing, and excitement shot quivering through me.

Well, to describe him as well as I may, from his wooden leg to the brown, fat hands which were folded over his stomach, would take a lot of time and many, many words. But what I think of, usually, is first of all the bloated body and face of the man which, somehow, went with the smile upon his face. His eyes were closed. He was either asleep or shamming it. No, I think that he was really asleep, and smiling when he thought of how he had digested the last living thing he caught in his web.

Next, I noticed the golden brown of his skin, with a hearty, healthy touch of red in the cheeks; and the grizzled hair which stuck up straight on his head in an unusual way; and the bald spot over one ear, the top of which was itself tattered as though a wild beast had worried it off. Then I think of his clothes, which were those of a vagabond, and finally, of the grease which blackened and shone upon the collar of his coat.

In any other setting, he would have been put down as a fat, worthless beggar—the sort of scoundrel who sits on a street corner and whines for pennies. But here it was very different. He was not whining. There were no whines in that pursed, smiling mouth of his. There were simply teeth.

The peon went over to his master, took off his straw hat, and made a bow.

"Swine!" said the sleeper, without opening his eyes.

What had wakened him, I wondered.

Apparently the crash of the closing front gate, like the boom of a cannon, had not been sufficient. He had slept through that. So could it have been no more than the trailing shadow of the peon's hat as it brushed across his face?

The peon bowed again, and then the fat man opened one eye and looked at me. I mean, deliberately, just that. He opened one eye, not both, and the eye which was opened was not filmed in the slightest. It was as bright and clear and keen as the eye of a boy. He kept that one eye open, and the other closed, while he stared at me.

The peon, having pointed me out, started to retire, but the

master said to him—in Mexican, of course, "Go get me a bottle of wine and two glasses, and be back here with them before I blink my eyes."

The peon disappeared. There was merely the shrill whisper of his huaraches on the stones, and I wondered if he feared the fat brute might mean what he said.

In the meantime, the master looked at me with both eyes; I would rather he had limited himself to one. He turned his fat head on his fat throat, slowly, as though there was a pivot joint which could be turned as a bird's is turned.

"How was the trip up?" said he, in good American, with a good American drawl to the words.

I could not have answered him. I was too astonished. I never saw a place where the American language seemed more out of place.

"Sit down," he went on, without waiting for me to speak. "Take that stool. The chair wouldn't hold you. Sit down and rest yourself."

I sat down on the stool, as directed. It was the cheapest, clumsiest sort of homemade manufacture—rudely shaped wood, held together by wrappings of sinews at the joints.

In this position, I faced him, and had the valley view behind me, also the sun. And I felt as though the whole valley was rising, and pouring swiftly toward me, like a river about to sweep me away.

It was a strange and giddy feeling, but I lost it almost at once. The reason I forgot about that odd sensation was that I saw my host was looking straight at me, with wide-open eyes—and yet he was directly facing the sun!

I don't think it was entirely an optical illusion. It seemed to me that I could see the terrible, keen ray of the sun enter his eye as it enters the eye of a snake. But this was not the flat lens of a snake's eye. This was brown, and the light shone deep inside it, running down a narrow, luminous well, as it were. However, he was not bothered. He continued to face that volleying of a million cruel lances without trouble, and I knew that he was not even dazzled, and that he was seeing me as clearly as though he sat in the shadow, and I in that blinding brilliance.

Then he said, "You know me, son? You know me, do you?"

"No, sir," said I.

Yes, like a boy I said it—a schoolboy.

"No, sir!" said I, to that vagabond, in his tatters, with his greasy collar and all, and his wooden leg, and his bloated stomach, round as the body of a spider that has dined well.

"I'm Pete Ruan," said he. "Pedro Ruan to the people in this little part of the world."

He waved his hand to indicate what he meant by "little part." The fences he indicated were the far, monstrous mountains. Inside of that range, I gathered mutely, was his domain. It was enough!

The peon came running back with the bottle and the cups. It was a leather bottle, of goat's hide, with the hair still on the outside. He held it under his arm, and he poured the red wine into wooden cups, hand-carved. They looked like mesquite wood, hard as ivory. I thought I saw the twisting grain of the mesquite root in them.

"It's a mighty bad wine," said Pete Ruan, "but you'll like it because it's cold. It's the temperature of spring water. Take a drink of that. It's not poisoned, either. Drink that and have a smoke. I'll send for her in a minute."

·7·

He kept on smiling as he talked. He moved nothing but his lips, and his fat cheeks quivered a little. From the moment he opened his eyes, his cheeks always seemed to be pulsating a trifle, as though he breathed with their power.

But what did he mean by sending for "her" in a minute? The fellow might be a wizard, a fiend. I was prepared to credit him any sort of power that could be imagined.

"Look here, Ruan—" I began. I stopped.

He sipped the wine. He sipped it noisily, and smacked his lips after he swallowed it.

"Horrible wine," he said. "But just the right temperature. Temperature of snow water that's run through the rocks. It's the only proper temperature for this climate. You can live on temperatures, son! Hot outside and cold inside, that's one good way. Or cold outside and hot inside. I get both degress, up here, summer and winter. How do you like that?"

I tried the wine. I was not at all sure that it was not poisoned, though I had just seen my host drink the very wine that I was sipping. It had rather a sharp, acrid taste; but there was some of the fruity taste of the grape in it, too; and as he said, it was cold, exactly the right degree of coldness for a man who had been riding all the day under the brilliant mountain sun.

"I like it," said I.

"Tell me your name," he demanded.

"I'm—well, José, in this part of the world, and Joe—"

"Never mind the last name," said he. "I just want a handle for you; that's all. How was the trip down?"

"Pretty good."

"How long?" said he.

"Ten days."

"Ten days—ten days," he murmured. "Mule, or horses?"

"One mustang," said I.

I was rather surprised to hear him asking so many questions. I half expected that he would know all about me and about every one else. He sipped his wine again, as loudly as before, and drew his big cheeks in, and let them unfold again, flowing down toward his shoulders.

"Yeah," said he. "That's quite a spell. Ten days of one mustang. That's thirty mile a day. That's three hundred mile. Eh?"

"Yes," said I. "Around about that, I reckon."

"Double the trail, make it about a hundred and fifty as the crow flies, eh?" said he.

"About that, maybe."

"You been educated. You can think better English than you talk, Joe," he said.

"I've been educated a little," I admitted.

"And then took your education and wasted it on a cow range, like me, eh?" said he.

I shrugged my shoulders. I kept feeling that he was driving at something important, though I could not quite make out what it might be.

"I done the same thing," said he. "I was educated, fine. Spanish and English. I took myself out West, and I wasted myself on the range, just the way that you've gone and done."

He smiled as he spoke. His complacence was enormous, and it was easy to see that he did not think that he really had wasted his time. No, he was satisfied with what he had done and what he had accomplished, even if the accomplishments included a wooden leg and the grease on his collar.

"It took a good while to learn the Western ways," he went on. "You know. Guns and things. They shot off a leg for me. Fine bright boy of Chicago, he shot my leg off, son. Pretty near didn't need a doctor. He put four bullets right through, side by side. He said he'd make me a lame duck and a tame one."

He put back his head. He opened his mouth. He closed his eyes. And he laughed, and his brown and rosy jowls shook up and down on either side of his mouth as he laughed.

It was like seeing a swine laugh.

I moistened my cracking lips and said nothing. I hardly thought, either. My mind was growing numb. A beastly fascination took hold upon me and kept my brain from moving.

"He was a good shot," went on Ruan. "He split the bone apart as clean as you ever seen. The doctor that came along a couple of days later and trimmed the leg off, he said that he hardly needed a saw, except to do a little trimming. He said that that shooting was purposeful shooting. And I admitted that it was. It was a good job that boy from Chicago did on me."

He had hardly finished laughing, as he said this. Gusts and rumblings of his enjoyment still were coursing through the vast hollow bulk of him, and his smiling lips puffed out his cheeks. I felt that he was smiling a good deal of the time simply to keep the fat of his cheeks back, as with two hands.

At the same time, I began to hate his smiling as much as I had hated his laughter. And I wondered how much good feeling toward Americans remained in him, after that little shooting escapade which had put him on one leg for the remainder of his life.

"I said I wasted myself on the range," he continued, "but it ain't a waste, when things like that happen to you. It's a lot different from a waste, I can tell you. I learned. You learn a lot while you're lying on the flat of your back with the life running out of your leg at every pulse of your heart. It's a great thing, son, to feel the clock running down, and nobody on hand to wind it up again. You ever feel that?''

I admitted that in such wisdom I was a novice.

"Ah, yes," says he. "I see how it is. Bein' so young, you're carryin' on to complete your education, some, and so you've come up here to take a look at me and my niece. Ain't that it?''

It was hard for me to answer. I tried to speak, but the words wouldn't come out. You can't very well walk into a house and tell the master of it—even if he wears a greasy collar—that you want to have a look at the beauty who is housed there.

But this Pete, or Pedro, Ruan, had no foolish delicacy about him. He sang out in a huge roar, "Lola! Lola!''

And I heard a faint answer, a sweet, small voice from the inside of the old house.

"You can have a look at her," said Ruan. "After the ride that you've taken, you can have a good, long look at her. I see that you're modest. Modesty's a foolish thing. There's many a man might have been king if he'd cared to go and sit on a throne. But if you keep yourself in the dust, you'll never get anything but pennies throwed to you, now and then!''

"Look here," said I, "you're not going to call out the señorita into the court just to—er—just to—I mean to say, Mr. Ruan, that you wouldn't want me to—''

"Here she is," says Ruan. He beckons. "Come right up, my dear," says he.

I got up from my chair with frost on my temples and cold fish down my back. I took off my hat and held it in both hands and tried to smile and look polite, and knew that I was gaping and grinning like a frozen monkey.

For there came Doloritas into the garden, stepping quietly among the broken rocks, and the wild brush. And she was the girl of the picture, mind you, only the picture didn't do her justice. Not by a reach a mile long. She was not big. She was only about shoulder-high on me. But I never liked a lengthy woman much. A man ought to have a chance to look down, in one sense at least.

As for the rest of Doloritas, I won't talk about her. I hardly dared to look at her face, though her eyes were down. I looked no higher than the hand with which she held together the filmy edges of her mantilla.

She came straight out there to us.

Then, as she paused, without looking up, Ruan says to her, "Maria, this is Don José. He's rode ten days to see you. Go and make him a bow."

She turned a little toward me and made the curtsey; but she did not lift her glance.

"He wanted to look you over," said Ruan, "and I reckon that you want to be looked. There she is, Joe. There ain't much to her, but what there is, is prime. She ain't big, but she's all quality. Look at that wrist. No bigger'n a baby's. Look at that hand, all dimples and softness, and not hardly big enough to hold a whip. But it can lift a mighty weight of trouble, d'ye see? Can't it, Maria?"

"Yes, señor," says she.

Oh, the soft, tired, musical voice of her. And the stony patience in her face as she submitted!

"Put out your foot, Maria," says he.

By heaven, she did it, actually lifting the hem of her skirt a little, and not a touch of color came into her pale, clear olive skin!

"Look at that pastern, Joe," said Ruan. "Look at the spring of it. Small, but made for speed, is what I always say about her. Look at that ankle, round as a bell. No big bone, no big tendons. A picture, is what she is. A real picture of a woman, is what my Maria is! But you ain't lookin', Joe!"

"Mr. Ruan," says I, "I don't think it—"

"Don't think, Joe," said Ruan. "That's the trouble with young men. They're always bound to be thinkin'. But don't you think. You just start in usin' your eyes and followin' your nose, and pretty soon you'll find yourself up on a high place. That's what I've done, and just look at where I am now!"

And he leaned back his head again, and opened his mouth, and closed his eyes, and once more, like a swine, he laughed; and I half expected something to strike him from the sky.

"It's Maria's fault," says Ruan, wiping the tears out of his eyes. "She embarrasses you a lot, not lookin' at you. Where's your manners, Maria? Look at the gentleman, will you?"

"Yes, señor," says she.

And she lifts her big brown-black eyes and looks at me. No, not really at me, but toward me, and past me, and into the big valley that makes me, I know, seem like a foolish pygmy in a great frame.

I could see that she was enduring as the martyrs endured in another day, with her soul and her mind shut to all physical sensations that could happen to her on this earth.

"That's better," says the brute, Ruan. "But it ain't good enough. Smile for the gentleman that's rode all this dusty way, Maria!"

• 8 •

NOW THAT I PUT DOWN THE WORDS OF THE ONE-LEGGED pig, it's sure hard enough for me to believe my hand that writes it and my eyes that see it; but the scene comes pouring back on me—the old garden, and the gleam of it in the sun, and the brown and rosy face of that pirate, Ruan, and the smile of the girl that seemed toward me, and for me, but was only for the world that lay behind me.

I looked down at the ground after one glance at her. I was pretty well done up by this submission to the outrageous orders of her uncle. And I would have given him a piece of my mind except that I told myself it would be foolishness to cross him. For nothing could be gained by that, whereas, if I said nothing, I might do something for Maria de los Dolores.

Only I most bitterly felt, now, that she had been rightly named, both for her beauty and her sorrows.

So she smiled when he directed, as she had looked toward me before, and extended her foot for my inspection, as a well-trained animal being offered for market.

This brute of a Ruan went on, "She's got a pretty lot of spirit, too. She ain't showin' herself off at all well, today. But she's got the right kind of a spirit in her, the sort of a spirit that a real Yankee likes. For I never seen an American yet that didn't like to have his womenfolks kick him in the face, now and then. Oh, she's got lots of heart in her. If you seen her reining a bucking mustang, or sitting a prancing young mule on the edge of nothing at all, or dancing here to a guitar. Why not dance now? By heaven, Maria, you shall dance now!''

He most excitedly clapped his hands and bellowed out something, but now I said, ''Mr. Ruan, I've never heard a girl spoken to like this before. I've heard enough of it, too. Let her be, won't you? If there's to be a dance, I'm not here to see it.''

He was not angered when I crossed him in this manner. He simply broke out once more in his loutish laughter. But I must say that the girl, who might have given me at least a direct glance in recognition of my interference, showed no emotion at all, and seemed as unconscious of me as before.

When his laughter had died off to a rumbling, he told me that it should be as I wished.

''Have you seen enough of her?'' he asked me.

Well, I couldn't say that. I could have looked at her, with a lot of pleasure, from that minute to this, and still been rooted there where I stood, I'll swear.

But I managed to say something about knowing that she was inconvenienced, and that I hoped she would do as she pleased.

At this old Ruan broke out with a roar, ''No, by Heaven, but she'll do what pleases you! That's all! She'll do what pleases you, my friend. You've come down here to risk your blessed neck for her, and now she'll please you, or she'll answer to me for it, and she'd better answer to the point!''

He put a lot of force and emotion into this. His eyes glared, I'll swear, with a red light, and his anger and fury were so great that after he had finished the words he lay for a while panting. There was no mask on him, now. He was all malevolence. He was all brute fury. What he had said I've only put down in part. Some of it was too full of cursing for me to repeat, because it makes my blood boil to think of the way I allowed him to speak in the presence of that girl—to her, in fact.

One thing was clear. He hated her with his entire, piggish nature!

He went right on at her. "Tell me, Maria," says he, "are you here to please the señor, or are you not?"

"I am here to please the señor," says she.

Some of her calm was gone, now. She was paler. Shadows were thumbed out under her eyes. I thought that I saw her lips trembling. Poor girl, she was suffering a good deal, and I was mightily sorry for her.

"If she's here to please me," I broke in, "she's free to go back to her room."

Ruan snorted and glared at me. Then he pointed.

"Get out of here!" he said to her. "He's told you to go, hasn't he? There's one more come here to suffer for your sake. And this one is telling you to get out of his sight. Why're you staying? Go, go!"

She didn't wait. But, by heaven, she gave him a little curtsey, and one to me, and off she went as meekly as you please.

I watched her with a tortured feeling that I should have done still more, and that I should have dressed down that swine of a Ruan. But there was another sting in me, and that was what he had said about me as "another come to suffer for her sake!"

I could imagine that this house might be an inferno. I thought that I had seen a bit of the Hades in it. But what, exactly, had become of the others who came here before me— for her sake?

It was enough to give any man pause for thought.

When she had gone, I was pretty well stunned, all things considered. I didn't know what to do or to say. I simply knew that I had been thrust into a false position.

At last, I saw that Ruan, the pig, was watching me with his brown and rosy smile, as cheerful as could be, and that he was waiting for me to speak.

So I gathered my courage and my wits as well as I could, and I said, "Señor Ruan, I'll tell you how it is—it's a true thing that I rode down here like a fool in an adventure book. And it's a true thing that it was because of Señorita Ruan that I came. But—''

"But what?" grunts the pig, though it continues smiling.

"But I see," said I, "that she never could care for—in other words, I wouldn't be wanted, and—''

"I want you, though," said Ruan. "You please me. That's what is important. This ain't an American household. This is Mexican, and it's the Mexican parents that decide who their children are going to marry. You please me. And you're gonna have my niece. You hear me?''

"I'll have to have something to say about that," said I.

I had gathered my dignity around me, you see, and felt rather Roman and even senatorial.

Ruan only laughed in my face.

"You've come here to get her," he said, "and you don't go away without her. Don't anger me, Joe, my son. My nephew, I should say, since that's what you're going to be. Now that you're inside of the house, you're not to leave until you have her, or until you're—''

He paused, and took another swallow of wine.

But he did not need to finish off his last speech, because I could supply the missing word. I was not to leave until I was the husband of the girl, or until I was dead!

You may say that it's not a great pressure to be forced to one's dearest wish. But I was all chills and fever.

He went on. "Sit down again."

I did as he told me.

"We're gunna be friends, my boy," says he. "As an enemy, I'm all thorns. But I can be a pretty good friend. Now wipe that fool look out of your face and talk to me sensible and open and manly and free!''

I took a breath, and settled myself on the stool as well as I could.

"Bein' friends," said he, "suppose you start right off and tell me about yourself.''

"I'll tell you whatever you ask," said I.

"It's easy for you to talk about yourself, is it?" said he.

"Yes," said I. "And afterward, will you tell me something about this place—and the men who've come before me?"

"Why, I might," said he. "If we're friends, words come easily to me. Now, suppose you tell me if you had any second reason for riding this far south."

"What?" said I.

"Outside of Maria, I mean," says he.

"No. What else could there be?"

He narrowed his bright, strange eyes at me.

"I mean," he explained, "that sometimes the law is fool enough to bother men—innocent men, of course—and make them want to get into a hole-in-the-wall country, just like this. But I don't suppose that the law ever has wanted you?"

I reflected back to a certain jail break in which I had assisted. But that matter had blown over. The law knew nothing, so far, to my discredit.

"No, the law has nothing against me," said I.

"Humph!" said he. And I felt that he was not exactly pleased.

He went on, "A boy with your education, Joe, and with everything that seems to be inside of you in the way of politeness, he's been well raised, and there's been some money behind him, and I guess that somewheres in the background, you got some rich relatives, ain't you?"

I smiled and shook my head.

"Not even a fifth cousin with an income worth leaving," I told him, truly enough.

He actually sighed with relief. His anxiety had pulled him forward in his chair, but now he relaxed deeply into it again. What evil was in him that made him glad that there was no great amount of money behind me?

"But you've got influential friends, anyway," he insisted. "I know the way that it is. You've got friends that can take care of you and push you along when the right time comes for the pushing!"

I shook my head.

"I don't even know a sheriff very well, except one," said

I. "No, I've got no influence. Now that I say that, I see that you think I'm a fool. I've come down here like a half-wit, hunting for—well, for Maria de los Dolores, and I have no way to provide for her, even if I should have all the luck, and win her. You're only right if you call me a blank fool. I see that for myself!"

No, I was all wrong.

He did not seem to be sorry that I was penniless and that I had no prospects in the world. Instead, he actually began to rub his fat hands together, so violently that even his brown-jelly cheeks were quivering with his pleasure.

And he beamed on me, and nodded at me again and again.

"Well, lad," said he. "I like to see a boy and a girl begin life right from the beginning, with a good start, and no money. And I'll be able to give you some advice. You can reach out and lean on me for millions of dollars in the way of advice, if you want to!"

I saw the thing clearly enough, now. Plainly he hated Maria, poor girl, so very bitterly that he was glad to see her married off to a beggar.

·9·

AFTER THIS, HE SEEMED TO LOSE INTEREST IN ME SUD-
denly. He clapped his hands twice, and a *moza* appeared, a
ragged wild cat of a woman with tousled hair streaming in
wisps across her face, and buried, hunted, desperate eyes.
He told her to take me to a room, and before I could get up
to leave him, I saw that the beast was asleep again, his eyes
shut, and his face composed; with the last fierceness of the
sun beating upon it, and the smile gently curving his lips.

Yes, there he was, sunk into a well of unpretended slum-
ber, with his hands folded caressingly upon his vast stomach,
while I went off behind the *moza*.

I felt that I had heard one profound truth from the lips of
Ruan. Even a swine could speak one truth, and say that this
place was Hades!

The *moza* went up before me, running on the stone stair-
way, which had been hollowed by many generations of use.
The ragged calico skirt whipped around her brown legs, as
corded with muscle as the legs of any peon who labors in the
mines or in the fields.

She took me up to the floor above and led me into a corner
room. It had a good prospect through two windows, one over
the eastern reach of the valley, and one straight up into the

southern mountains. But view was about all that room could offer. There was a cot with a goatskin over it and a straw pallet—and no other bedding whatever! And there was a worn and faded grass mat on the floor, and one stool like the one on which I had sat in the garden below. There was also a homemade table, very small, and a wooden bowl on it, and a bucket of water beside it, and a coarse towel thrown over the top of the wooden bowl.

Here was the total equipment to receive a guest, and I had little doubt that this was as good accommodation as one could expect to receive in the house.

Well, of course I had roughed it in worse quarters than this. But what I looked suddenly toward was the picture of Doloritas, delicate, slender, frail, and all the sorrow of her name standing in her eyes. She of all living creatures to be raised up in such a house as this!

I turned back from the window toward the *moza*, who was standing in the door. She had not been waiting to receive my orders, but had lingered there, it appeared, to have another glance at me. For now I saw her finishing her survey, without hurry, and something between a sneer and a grin on her face.

I never saw or received a more evil glance than this in all my life, except once!

She did not banish her grin when she saw that she was observed. Only, presently, she shrugged her lean, muscular shoulders and withdrew, and went down the outer hall with the springing step of a young athlete, rather than that of a matron of some forty-odd winters.

I sat down on the casement and smoked a cigarette and tried to think matters over. But, to save my life, I could not manage it. For it seemed to me that I was merely more definitely than ever committed inside the frame of a picture, and that like any other production of the artist who had put me in, I possessed no authority or governance over my own actions.

What was to be done with me would be done, and I could fold my hands and wait.

In spite of this inward observance, rather naturally I could not calm myself, and I smoked my cigarette so fiercely that I burned my lips with it before I was aware.

So I threw it away and spent a moment running over the mechanism of my revolver. It was new, and it shot strongly and well, as most Colts do. I was not a bad hand with it. But as I sat there in the casement, it seemed to me that I had been the most careless jackass in the world and that the manifest duty of every human was to spend at least an hour a day in the use of firearms.

I had not spent that hour. I had neglected my opportunities. Now I should, perhaps, need to use weapons as an artist uses a musical instrument, and I should be found lacking in the moment of need!

Well, there was no point at all in sitting still and mourning about calamities which, at least, had not yet happened. So I left my room and started exploring the house a little. But it was such a jumble that I needed a guide to make head or tail of it. I very soon got into the ruined part of it, and there it was plain that I had guessed rightly. What had knocked it about was a force that burst on the inside, for the walls leaned back, and the fragments of the roof did not lie on the floors of the despoiled rooms. The whole roof here seemed to have been blown off, and there was a blackened pit from which the explosion appeared to have come.

I looked at this thing with an increased trouble. The whole house seemed filled with gloominess.

Then I followed the remnants of a broken staircase out of that blackened pit and so up to the roof of the house.

This was much better. Even where the roof had fallen in, there was a broad rampart remaining at the sides, though the surface of it was much broken, of course. One could make the big circuit of the house itself and all about the walls, even the walls of the patio, to the gates. That was the walk I took, and found the gates still closed, and outside of them, I looked down at a ragged shepherd who was squatted on a rock, but instead of a crook, he was leaning on an old rifle. My shadow from the wall brushed across him, and he looked up quickly.

Like all the others who were connected with the place,

when he first saw me, he gave me a sinister and foreboding grin. Then, slowly and deliberately, he took off his straw hat and saluted me; but he did not rise. There was a good deal of mockery, I thought, in that courtesy of the peon's.

"If you wait long enough down there," I said to him, "a deer may walk up and wait for you to shoot it."

He grinned back at me. He showed me his long rows of white teeth, and his nostrils flared a little, as the cheek muscles pulled at them.

"Even a bear might come, señor," said he.

"Yes," said I, "even a bear. That's pretty strong meat, but there's lots of it."

"Or a mountain lion might come," went on the guard.

"Yes, or a mountain lion," said I.

"And jump even this wall, señor?" said he. His eyes flashed significantly at me.

"Jump the wall to steal chickens?" I asked.

"Hai!" said the man, more excited than ever. "You don't know about the mountain lions that we have about here?"

"No. I don't know about them," said I. "You tell me, my friend."

"Yes," said he, "as I am your friend, I must tell you. It is this. The mountain lions all around us in these hills, they have a strange appetite, señor. The flesh that they like the best is the flesh of gringos!"

His sneer was filled with the most deliberate malice.

"They must be very thin cats," said I, sarcastically.

"No," said the peon, "they are fat—but the diet makes them mangy!"

I felt like climbing down and punching his round, brown face for him. There's nothing that can be as insolent as a Mexican, when the humor strikes him.

However, I saw that there was no use trying to get down that wall, and still less use in inviting him to come up and argue the point with me. Americans were not popular in this corner of America. That was simply all that there was to it.

"You know, amigo," I said to him, "that every hole is not a rat hole?"

"I have heard that," said he.

"And," said I, "while you sit there and watch for the mouse, perhaps a snake will come out and taste all of you at one bite."

He rubbed the lock of his rifle with affectionate hands, as he heard me say this. And still he sneered, and grinned, and looked spitefully up to me.

"I have killed snakes, too," said he. "I always blow their heads off, because the fools cannot help pointing themselves down the gun barrel!"

I could not help laughing a little. I mean to say, this man's malice was so open and his hatred of the "gringo" was so sincere that it stopped being offensive. It was a caricature.

When I laughed, he actually opened his mouth and gaped at me. He seemed amazed by my mirth. But, after a moment, he shut his mouth again and began nodding his head, as one who understands.

"The sheep are that way, too," said he again.

"What way?" I asked.

"Happy even in the slaughterhouse," said he.

It was a little more than my nerves could stand. I glowered for a moment at him. He was grinning once more, triumphant at having caught me so easily. Then I got my dignity together as well as I could and marched off from him.

I circled back on the rampart.

The view straight down, on all sides except that of the gates, was a pretty dizzy thing. In one place, I dare say, that the almost sheer drop amounted to something like a hundred yards down to the floor of the valley. This great height made the big old house seem smaller, perched rather lightly on its crag.

From the added height, too, I had a good view of the entire valley, and could mark every twist of the creek. It was running rose and gold, now, until it carried all of its color and brightness into the blue mists at the foot of the valley, where a gorge slit sharply, like an ax cut, through the mountains that were ranged there. It was an odd thing to imagine the millions of years that that trickle of water must have consumed cutting through such a mass of solid rocks!

The mountains, now that I was held up among them, as it were, took more of my attention than the plain. A wild lot were those peaks. They had a raw look, as though their bare heads had just been heaved up from the sea level the day before and they were still glittering with the salty water, though they had picked up some forests upon their shoulders in rising. From the western peaks, flags of clouds streamed out in long pennons that snapped off at the ends and kept shooting volleys of little fog puffs across the blue.

I watched them with fascination, for the sunset was coloring them all, and each one differently.

The wind was growing colder, rapidly. A damp chill was in it, and I felt that it was the breath of the oncoming night. I had a foolish thought of how far night had to creep up from the dark world before it could master this height, and as I turned from looking upward toward the bright sky, I saw that Doloritas was standing there before me, precariously near the verge of the rampart.

· 10 ·

NOW, WHEN MY EYE WAS TAKEN SO SUDDENLY FROM THE hugeness of the mountains, and the sweep of the clouds in the wind, and brought down to the single form of the girl, she seemed to me a child, and I most certainly a fool and a brute for coming here to pursue her.

I got off my hat and went up to her, and though I thought that I could see her wincing away from me a little, there was so much fine courtesy in her that she met me with a smile and a little inclination of her head and body that was almost another curtesy.

I said to her, "Señorita Maria, will you listen to me a little?"

"Don José," says she, "I came up here to talk to you if I could." She blushed a little, as though there were some guilt in this. And then she went on, "There's no other place where we could talk safely together, but here the wind will blow our words away as fast as they are spoken."

It was an odd way of putting it. One might have thought that words were concrete substances, likely to fall like leaden bullets, or images which could be picked up and afterward read by others.

It put a good deal of heart in me to have her begin in this

fashion, so I said, "Your uncle goes about things in a very harsh sort of a way. I don't want you to understand me as being of a mind with him."

The fear seemed to be quite out of her. She looked at me rather with pity and curiosity.

I went on. "You know, Maria, that I came down here—to—er—"

I stuck on this. The girl astonished me by coming to my help.

"You came down here because you saw a picture of me, and you saw that I had a pretty face," says she. And there was no boldness or immodesty in her saying. Instead, she was not even coloring. She put up her slim hands to the sides of her head, as though she were measuring and making small the face of which she had been speaking.

"Yes," said I. "That's the reason of it. But you know, Maria, that a man thinks that he can see something besides prettiness in some faces. I don't want to rush along into compliments and make a fool of myself before I know you. But that's the truth, and—"

She lifted a hand to stop me.

"There's no reason to apologize for saying anything to me," said the girl. "My uncle will have us dead or married inside of twelve hours, I think. If he can drag us to it."

That silenced me.

She went on, "And there's nothing that either of us can do about it. You cannot get away, now that you've been closed into the house, unless some one shows you how to get out of the place. And there's only one person who will show you how to manage that."

"Who is that?" said I.

"I will do it," said she.

A good hot wave of romantic hope jumped up in me.

"You want to escape from the house with me, Maria?" said I.

She smiled sadly at me.

"What good would it do for me to try to run away? He would catch me."

"After all," said I, "your uncle has a wooden leg, and we might be able to go as fast as his hired men."

"My uncle?" said the girl. "No, no! I'm not speaking of him. I mean that other one, who can climb these walls as a squirrel climbs a little tree!"

"What other?" said I.

She gaped at me, and putting out her hand, she rested it on the top of the wall and seemed to need that support.

"Good heavens," says she, "do you tell me that you came down here without knowing about him?"

"Not a word," said I. "I know nothing. I only know the picture of you, and yourself and your uncle as I've seen you. That's about my limit of knowledge, Maria. I've tried to guess a good deal, but I haven't managed very much."

She looked about her in a desperate way, as a person does when there's a great explanation to offer, and no words in which to put it.

"Tell me this, señor," says she. "Was it a friend of yours who showed you my picture?"

I thought back to Chip. He was a queer boy, but I would have banked his friendship, or his good faith, at least, against a million.

"Yes," said I, "a friend!"

She cried out: "You're wrong! He's a lying friend, and a man who wants to see you dead, or he never would have sent you here."

I was falling into a panic again, rather naturally, but there are limits past which most of us won't be driven in fear, at least, in the daytime. Now I shrugged my shoulders. I said, "Look here, Maria. It seems that somewhere in the mountains, there's a lion of a man—"

"Ah, yes," says she. "A lion!"

"And he's going to come in here and eat me alive. Is that it?"

"What can keep him from it?" she answered, putting out both her hands, palms up.

That answer was sufficiently naïve. It was sufficiently convincing, too.

But I remained logical.

"There are the walls," said I, "for one thing."

"He will climb them as if they were a low board fence," says Doloritas.

"And then there is your uncle and his servants, who seem a tough lot," said I.

"They will run from him as mice run from a cat," said she. "Besides, I think they love him. They serve my uncle. I don't know why; but they would serve that other because they love him."

"Well, then," said I, "supposing he's come through everything else, and he lands here, there's still me, isn't there? I'm not a great hero, but I can put up some sort of a fight!"

She watched me, and nodded.

"You are brave, señor," says she.

"Not so brave, either," said I. "But will you tell me, Maria, if I have some sort of a hope—if there's a hope possibly in front of me, supposing I should win through this fight, with whoever it may be?"

"A hope of what?" said she, frowning, and a little bluntly.

"Of you," said I, equally bluntly.

"No," said she, and slowly shook her head.

This bluntness of hers angered me a good deal this time, and I said, "Well, there's always that hope remaining—that your uncle will drag us together, as you say, and marry us off."

She did not even flush.

"You would be dead within an hour afterward," says she.

"I don't think so," said I. "Another thing, Maria. What makes you so sure that no one could have a chance with you? Let me have the right to ask you if you've promised yourself to any other man?"

"No," said she.

"And then what locks you up so?" said I.

"I never shall marry," says the girl.

"Hello," said I, "that's a pretty young way of talking! You're a man hater, then. Is that it, Maria?"

She smiled away from me in a singular manner, at the mountains and the moving, rosy sky.

"No," said she. "I hate no one. But I've seen enough of men!"

She broke out at me, then, "Don't you suppose that I have a reason for what I'm saying? Do you think I'm talking only to draw you on, farther and farther? Oh, I tell you that I've seen reasons as red as the best blood in your heart, señor!"

She pointed down. I could conjure up dead men at her feet. And her face was pale and tragic.

I must say that during this little talk she seemed to have drawn a great distance away from me. I felt that she was a very superior being, and that I was hardly worthy of kissing the ground at her feet. But I also felt that there was nothing in the world half so worth having as herself.

"You won't ask for reasons any more, señor," says she. "You understand now that I mean what I say, and that you are to forget me? And tonight I'll come quickly after darkness and show you the way from your room. Are you a brave climber? Are you not afraid of great heights, and climbing with a rope?"

"I should say that I'll go," I admitted sullenly.

"You will say so," remarked the girl, very sure of herself. "You are not so young as some of the others," she added gloomily.

"I should say that I'll go," says I. "But the fact is that the more you convince me with your talk. Maria, the giddier I'm getting in the wits. I ought to do as you say. You don't care a whit about me. You probably never will. But all the same, I can't pull myself away. You starve a cat long enough, Maria, and it'll sneak into the kitchen and stay there, no matter how hard you beat it."

This girl came suddenly up to me and threw well back the hood that the wind was sweeping about her, and let the flow of the air press her clothes about her as closely and smoothly as though she had been suddenly drenched in water. And she held out her arms to me, and raised her face in a way that I never can forget, and she said, "Look at me, señor!"

"Heaven knows, Maria," said I, "that I am looking with all my heart!"

"But you're not seeing the truth," says she. "You're only seeing this instant, and you don't know what will be left of me five years from now, or how I'll be scored and marked and bent and writhen. Oh, Don José," says she, and begins to cry like a child, "I'm not what you think. I'm not proper for you to look at, as you're looking now. You had better take home a curse with you than to take home me!"

I don't know what I should have done or said—except that I must have told her that I would welcome a thousand times over a curse wearing her face, but just then a loud voice which had both a boom and a ring to it shouted up from the center of the house, as if out of the bowels of the earth, "Doloritas!"

She shrank. She snatched the cloak about her as though to hide herself.

"I must go!" said she, her frightened eye lingering on me a last and desperate instant. "Heaven give you wisdom. Heaven give you strength. Pray for us both, as I shall pray!"

And off she went, and the bull-bellow of Ruan rose and roared and rang again, calling for her.

· 11 ·

I HAD SUPPER WITH RUAN, OUTSIDE THE HOUSE, IN A COR-
ner of the patio. The gate had been thrown open, and we
could look out through it toward the end of the day. As the
dusk grew thicker and thicker, big torches—the most primi-
tive kind, made of resinous pine wood—were brought out and
kindled. Four of them flamed and snapped and cast out daz-
zling yellow sparkles, while the black smoke went shooting
up above their heads.

They made a wild company, from my point of view. And
they cast a proper kind of light over the brutal face of Ruan.

The girl was not with us, and when I asked after her, he
said with his smile that she was tired, after her chat with me.

"You take a woman that has to talk agin' a high wind,
like that," said Ruan, "and it tires her a lot, eh? Particular
when all her talk goes for nothing. I've got a little disappoint-
ment of my own to tell you about."

I asked what it could be, and he said, "Why, the good,
honest, fat brown padre—he looks enough like me to be my
brother—ain't coming here, tonight for the marriage."

"Ill?" said I.

"Likely," answered Ruan. "He ain't to be found, at least.
He's gone and disappeared! That's what our mountain lion

has managed, this time. But then, he always has his little tricks. Always a trick here or a trick there. A cat's a mighty smart beast, son, and it takes a wakeful man to beat it!''

Well, I could agree heartily enough to that.

I said, "What's the name of this fellow—this lion—this wildcat that every one talks about so much?''

"Oh, he has a lot of names," said Ruan. "He has so many names that it likely wouldn't do much good if I was to tell you about 'em! You eat your supper and go to bed early, and have a good sleep. The morning'll be the time for you and Maria! She done her best to talk you down, I reckon?''

I avoided his face. I could not bear to see his grin as he spoke to me of the girl.

"She did her best," said I. "Nobody could do more than she did! What my position ought to be, I don't know. I'm pretty well baffled.''

"I'll tell you your position," said Ruan, calmly. "Your position is between the devil and the deep blue sea. The devil is the pretty face of the girl that you want. The deep blue sea is conscience. Conscience is always putting up a fight for us to get us into heaven, and conscience is always losin' the fight. You go up to bed and don't you bother no more about your worryin'. You'll do what any man would do, when the time comes. You'll take the girl, and spend a week or two thankin' fortune that you've got her. Besides, the fact is that she don't know much about men, son. You take that fact in mind, and you'll see that kindness and all that would pretty soon make her fond of you. Them that marry out of love are in the worst way. There's no place for them to go except downhill. And that's the fastest and the worst way to go. But them that marry just by agreement, why, they've got no place to go except up—which is fine for the view—or straight ahead on the level, which is the easiest way of all.''

He seemed in a humor to talk a great deal, but I had had enough of him for that occasion. I left the table, as he suggested, and went up to my room, where I sat gloomily by the light of a bad-smelling, homemade candle. The candle soon melted down into its little stone basin, and the wick, hanging over the lip of the basin, continued to burn, or rather, to fume—giving only a treacherous glimmer of light in the room.

I knew very well that I could not sleep, so I lay down and tried to think things out, and find something worth while in my thoughts. But all I could do was to repeat, like one hypnotized, the words of Ruan, when he said that I was between the devil and the deep blue sea. Yes, that was very true indeed. I was between the devil and the deep blue sea. And the devil, as he had suggested, was more than reasonably sure to win.

While this was going on in my mind, I forgot even the words of Ruan, and lost myself in watching the waves of shadows as they washed back and forth across the ceiling of the room.

Well, I was about as unhappy and worried as a man can be. I was worried because I felt that I was being drawn into a dastardly role, and I was frightened because of that unnamed fellow who, like a wild cat, roamed through the mountains and, it seemed, could not be kept from leaping into this house and carrying away living men like mice between his jaws.

I wriggled at the thought, and as I wriggled, I heard something between a sigh and a groan in my room.

I could not even sit up. I was frozen too stiff for that. And then I remembered that like a jackass I had left my revolver upon the chair and not taken it with me when I stretched on the bed. I was helpless. There was not a weapon within my grasp!

I heard the same sound repeated, and then it seemed to me that it was not actually in the room, but just outside—at a window—no, at the door, perhaps.

I heard it again. It was the same moaning sound which I had listened to before, and now I felt a return of courage. Things that sigh and moan were not what I would essentially fear. I got up from the bed, caught hold of my revolver and tiptoed to the door, listened, and thought that I heard the faint whisper of breathing just outside of it.

"Who's there?" said I.

"Pierce Collins, about all in. Open the door and give me a hand, will you?"

This might be a mere ruse to get my door open, of course, but the gasp of the speaker was sufficient to reassure me. It's the sound that comes out when a man is sick with pain.

I pulled my door open, and by the shaking light from my room's lamp, I saw a long fellow sprawled upon the floor of the hall. He was struggling to his hands at the moment, and I leaned over him.

"Get me into your room," said he. "Get me onto a bed and covered up. The cold of the stones is biting through me like teeth. I thought I was gunna die here like a fish out of water. Take me in for mercy's sake, will you? I came here to do you a good turn, and now it's like to be the death of me!"

I could not help believing in him. I leaned over, got a good grip under his shoulders, and pulled him like a sack into my room, and dragged him onto my bed in the same fashion.

Then I hurried back to close that door to the hall, for it seemed to me that all sorts of dangers were running with a tiptoe whisper of speed to get at me through that opening.

I closed, and locked, and bolted, the door and braced the stool against it. Then I came back to Pierce Collins.

He lay exactly where I had left him, his arms flopping clumsily at his sides, a faint pucker between his eyes, and his lips working a little.

Yes, he felt pretty sick. There was no doubt about that.

I thought he was a mighty good-looking fellow, of the thin-faced and long-drawn-out type. But he seemed to be cut clean, and cut right. I put a hand over his heart. It went fast and fluttering, but there was no real stagger to him, and I guessed that he was not so badly off as he thought. So I said, "Look here, Collins, you're better than you think. You're gunna be all right."

"Thanks, old son," said he, in something better than a whisper. "I guess I'll be better. When I slipped and fell in the hall, I thought that the strain had busted the wounds open again. Feel under my coat. Is there any blood running?"

That gave me a bit of a jar, all right. But I felt under his coat and it was all dry across his breast. I found where the broad, thick bandage went right around it.

"Somebody got you pretty close to the wick," I suggested to him. "But there's no blood running now. You're dry as a board."

"Thank heaven," said he. "Yes, I was trimmed; I was pretty nearly put out. But that's all right, too. I feel better, now that I know the blood didn't start. My gosh, partner, how it takes it out of a fellow to think that the blood has started!"

I could see that Pierce Collins was no hero. But neither am I, so it didn't matter so much.

He went on, "Bend a little closer. I want to save my strength all I can. I have to get back down that hall, pretty soon, to my room. I've come here to give you a tip, old son. Will you take it?"

"I ought to," said I, "after you've spent so much trouble to get here. What's the tip about?"

"Doloritas!" said he.

I grunted, the name hit me so close to home.

"Yeah," said he, seeming to recognize the sound that I had made. "I was that way about her. Until I got tapped with a .45-caliber slug! And that let out all the romance, I tell you."

"You came here because of her?" said I.

"Yes," said he.

"Did a kid go and fetch you?" I asked.

"A kid? What kid? What sort of a kid would go and fetch me?" he asked, puzzled.

"It's nothing," said I. I was relieved to see that Chip was not a mere rat catcher. "You came here account of Maria— and this is what happened to you. How thick were you with the girl?"

"Not with her at all," says he. "I fixed it up Mexican style with her father. That's the Mexican way, you know. I fixed it up with him, for me and Doloritas. Everything went along pretty well—"

"What did the girl think?" said I.

"They don't think much, Mexican girls," said Collins. "They let their families do the fixing for them. It's not a bad way. They get on pretty well, afterward, it looks to me. Only this time, nobody counted on the other one."

"What other one?" said I.

"El Blanco," says he.

"Who is that?" I asked.

"Who—is—that?" says he, letting his voice rise with each word a little. "Why, El Blanco is the original fiend. That's what he is! And he's a fiend that wants Maria de los Dolores, and he jumped the wall of this here house when he heard what I was after—and this is what happened to me. And that's why I come dragging down the hall to let you know. He'll jump the wall for you, too. And you won't turn out as lucky as I did."

A door banged in the distance. I jumped halfway across the room when I heard it. Then I hurried back to my wounded man.

"He'll murder any man who wants Maria?" said I. "But he didn't murder you!"

"No, because I knuckled under," said Collins. "And I swore to him that I'd never look at her again. And now you come, poor chap, and you're between El Blanco and Ruan— and heaven help you, and heaven help the girl, too!"

· 12 ·

EVEN BEFORE THIS, I HAD NOT BEEN FEELING PARTICU-
larly chipper. Now I felt a good deal worse, naturally. At last
I said to him. "Did the girl ask you to do this?"

"What?" he muttered.

"To come here and tell me these things?"

"Yes," said he. "She's pretty decent. She's like you, between the fear of El Blanco and Ruan, her uncle."

"What makes him want to see her married off?" I asked.

"Don't you know that?" asked Collins.

"No, I can't imagine, except that he's such a fiend that he
doesn't want her around the house with him."

"The house won't be his until she's married. That's the
terms of the will his brother made when he died."

"Was her father worried about getting her married off?"
I asked. "Why, she could find a husband in every block of
a big city."

"A white American husband, though, is not so easy to
come at, down here," said Collins. "They have to be fetched
in, you might say."

"Just how were you fetched in?" I asked.

"Oh, I was down here doing some honest prospecting.
That was all. I just happened to see her and her uncle to-

gether, when they were out riding. Everything flowed out of that like water running downhill. You know how it is!''

I thought of the beauty of the girl, and it seemed to me that the whole world would follow if it saw her.

''You'll not be a fool, man,'' said Collins, urging me on. ''You'll let the girl show you out from the house tonight, won't you?''

''This fellow, this El Blanco,'' said I, ''is he as much poison as all that?''

''There's no more poison in the world!'' said Collins, very heartily. ''He's all out by himself! And a cold-blooded devil, too. If he found me here in your room, he'd cut my throat along with yours and—''

Collins had talked himself into a thoroughgoing panic, by this time; he seemed to feel that El Blanco, like a cat, was walking right into the room. I had a good deal of the same feeling, myself, but his terror, instead of being contagious, sobered me and steadied me a little.

I told him that I was mighty grateful for the warning he gave me, and that now the first thing was to get him back to his room. So I took him under the armpits and helped him into the hall. A gust of wind came down it with a rush and a chilly whisper, and Collins wilted in my arms, and moaned. But I managed to hold him up until he had made the two or three turns necessary to get to his room.

It was a duplicate of mine for barrenness, but it was long and narrow as a tunnel, with one window, like a single eye, looking down through the length of it. Collins peered about fearfully at it as though he were seeing it for the first time; but finally he nodded, as though to admit that it might be his apartment. I got him over to his bed and he lay down, shuddering and groaning, and muttering that he wished he never had seen the cursed house of Ruan.

I could have seconded that wish, except for Doloritas. So I went slowly out of that room and down the hall toward my own room. Enough moonlight to show the way slanted through the windows, but in spite of that, I lost my direction—I think it was because I must have gone down instead of up a certain flight of steps. At any rate, all at once I walked straight out into the old, ruined garden!

I had a cold feeling that my fate had brought me there; it was like being pushed onto a stage before an audience which I still could not see; and it seemed to me that the moon was pouring down the sweet, thin odor of jasmine. As for the garden itself, between sun and moonlight it was transformed. The wrinkles, one might say, had gone out of it, and it presented a young and lovely face.

I went over to the parapet that looked east down the valley. To the west, the plain was as clearly printed out as at noonday; but here to the east the moon mist clouded everything from side to side.

Sometimes the river flashed a bright curve through this luminous fog, and sometimes the rocks were glinting, but on the whole there was little to be seen here.

I remember thinking that, after all, a man's life was something like this, and even the brightest parts of it were clouded over, let's say, with too much light, and the true facts of it came flashing through in mere bits and moments. I grew more and more the fatalist. If I were to die here in the house of Ruan, why, I would die, and that would be an end of it. I took a good grip on the handle of my Colt, and that made me feel better. As for El Blanco, he was only mortal. And if I could hit a rabbit—now and then—I might also be able to hit a man!

I was being logical, you see, and there's nothing in the world so dangerous as logic; it leads you into pits a mile deep.

Now I saw something flutter from the corner of my eye, and I turned about and saw Maria de los Dolores coming toward me. Not that I knew her at first, for she wore a widebrimmed riding hat and the rest of her was swallowed up in a big cloak. But when a woman once has touched a man's heart, she cannot come near without stirring it like music again. So I knew her even before I could penetrate through the thick black of shadow that fell across her face. She paused by the dead fountain, and her gesture in drawing her cloak closer about her shoulders made me sure of her.

I went over and met her. I said, "Look here, Doloritas, you ought not to be wandering about alone at night in this house."

"But you see, señor," says she, "I am not alone."

And, with a charming gesture, she indicated me, and drew me into her company and her intimacy. It jumped my heart over a mountain and brought it down singing. I moved a little closer to her and made sure that she was actually smiling a little.

"Doloritas," said I, "you've come out here to see me. About what?"

"To take you out of the house," said she. "To take you out before he comes!"

"El Blanco?" said I. "I don't care if he comes riding a dragon. I'm going to stay here. I was doubting myself, a while back, but now I've seen you smile. And I'm staying here. I wouldn't budge without you!"

"Look," says she. "I am dressed for riding!"

I caught her by the arms; I turned her toward the moon, and she bent her head back a little and let me see her smile.

"By the eternal jumping thunder, my dear," said I, "do you want me to guess that you care a little about me?"

She said nothing. She only opened her eyes and looked up at me. And that was enough to make my head swim. I took her in my arms. I held her until I could feel the warmth of her body and the beat of her heart. Then I leaned and kissed her lips. They were cold, and a small shudder went through her, but she did not draw away.

I asked myself if the shudder were on account of my nearness; but then I decided that this could not be, for she made no effort to escape. It was a miracle that she could care for a common, plain-faced man like me. But no matter what a pagan a man may be, when it comes to love, he puts his trust in Heaven and is willing to believe in miracles.

I believed in this one.

"If you will ride with me, Doloritas," I said, "I'll go

now, and I'll keep on riding to the end of the world with you. Shall we go now?''

"I'm ready," said she.

"Then lead me as far as the horses, and after that, I'll gladly lead in my turn."

She turned away from me without a word, but looking back over her shoulder toward me with that faint, cold smile which had half maddened me with joy before. Oh, women are fools when their smiles grow too broad! All that they need to do is to touch a man with a single glance.

We did not cross through the patio, at all. Instead, we went back from the garden and down a few twists of stone steps, some of them moist and slippery, until we reached, in this way, a place that seemed far underground. And here we found a complete stable with nine or ten horses and mules tethered. My roan was among them, and when it got the wind of me, it greeted me with a whinny that sounded like a growl from a dog.

However, I was mighty glad to see it again. I asked the girl what she would ride and what I should saddle for her, but I was surprised to see that she was already leading out a mule, ready saddled and bridled.

It gave me a slight shock. It seemed to imply, in a stroke, that she was entirely sure of her power, and that before she so much as spoke to me, she had made all of her preparations for the flight.

But I was not in a humor to be too critical. Whatever she wished to do would be well done, in my eyes.

She pointed out a sliding door which must be opened. So I pushed it out, and it made a faint, thunderous rumbling that chilled my nerves.

She passed through; and as she passed, looking up at the sheer height of the wall of masonry, I heard her say, "Heaven forgive me!"

"Forgive you for what, Maria?" I asked her.

But she did not hear me, or at least, she did not seem to hear me; and I, in the meantime, was closing that sliding door again, and thanking heaven that we had got clear so easily. All of those armed guards, set to keep out the wild-cat attacks of El Blanco, had not been able to prevent our departure—wild and careless crew that they were!

But still we were under the brow of peril.

The door had opened at the base of the hill on which the house of Ruan stood, and now we had directly before us the moon mist of the eastern valley.

As we rode out, down the easy pitch of the slope toward the plain, I looked back for a farewell glance to the lofty old house, and its immense bastions, and as my eye ran up the line of the wall, I saw in an open casement, like a picture painted in black and white, the face, the thick shoulders, and the folded arms of Ruan himself!

No one can tell what a shudder the thing cast through me. If he had had a rifle at his shoulder, ready to fire, that would have been as nothing, compared to the vast, placid, evil smile on his face. And the mere folding of his fat arms seemed to tell me that, no matter how far I went, how hard I rode, I still would be simply executing the will of the master of the house, and would never get beyond his power.

• 13 •

THE GIRL WAS A LITTLE IN THE LEAD. I HURRIED TO CATCH up with her.

"He's watching us, Doloritas!" I whispered to her. "Ride faster!"

"Oh, fast horses or sure-footed mules will do us no good now," said the girl, wonderfully steady. "Ride straight on, José. There is no danger behind us. All the danger is in front!" She waved before us.

I was utterly amazed by her calm. I asked her, "Do you know a safe place to make for?"

"There are friends I can trust in the town of San Jacinto," said the girl. "If we can get there, we are perfectly safe. There are such friends in San Jacinto that not even El Blanco will dare to make trouble." She tossed back her head in a way that I was to remember, later on, and there was a sort of fierce triumph in her voice. "There are such friends in San Jacinto that they would tear out the claws of the tiger, one by one!"

She made a fierce gesture, while I watched, amazed at her emotion.

"He has walled me up in that horrible old house—even

my uncle was no match for him. But now I trust that you will match him, José!''

She reached out and laid her hand on my arm, and she leaned somewhat toward me with a smile that might have opened gates of iron—to say nothing of my poor soul!

I said, ''Did your uncle consent to let you go, tonight? He told me that you would stay, and I would stay until—''

''That was what he always was saying,'' she answered, ''until I pleaded with him. And I swore that one day El Blanco would jump into the house and carry me off like a mouse between his teeth. And then what of all the plans of my uncle? El Blanco has laid his power like two great arms around our house. Half of our servants are his spies. He has corrupted the people who work in the fields. Every one works for him. There was no one to trust!''

She gave a shivering moan. Then, sweeping her hand to this side and to that, she went on. ''We lived on a wretched little island in the midst of a great river. That was the power of El Blanco. And then came that weak man—that Señor Collins—that coward and fool!''

I gaped when I heard her.

''Oh, but after all,'' said I, ''Collins wanted to help you all he could. You're pretty hard on him, Maria!''

Well, as I said this, I could see her eyes burn at me.

''He surrendered to one man!'' said she. ''Only a dog would do such a thing as that. He surrendered to one man. He begged for his life. What is the life of such a creature as that worth, I ask you, José?''

I found that this was a little bit hard to answer, to tell the truth. For, you see, there was a ring and a force in the voice of Maria de los Dolores that staggered me. I thought that this force gave strength and character to her, no doubt; but I also thought that it loaned her a touch of hardness, and I could not help remembering that there are bullfights and other cruelties in Mexico. But, after all, one must not criticize in the individual the faults of a nation.

''Well, Doloritas,'' said I, ''you may rate Collins low; but

I might have done exactly as he did. I'm no hero. And that's not modesty, either!''

She turned her head and watched me, and said not a word. I grew mighty uncomfortable in the pause, I can assure you!

''You would do more for me, José!'' said she, at last. ''Now is the time for us to ride. Even my uncle felt that there might be good fortune lodged in you. You must ride, now.''

She set the example by striking her mule with her heels, and that mule began to run as I never had seen a mule run before. Usually, they have a short, jerking gait. They are made for walking or for a short-stepping jog trot. But this animal could gallop freely.

The roan, of course, kept up without any trouble; but after twenty minutes of stiff going, the roan was feeling the pace more than the mule.

Doloritas rode very well. All her people have a gift for work in the saddle, and she was not an exception. The cloak blew streaming from her shoulders; the wind of the gallop pressed against her; but still, over rough or smooth, she was able to turn and give a long regard to the distance in which the house of Ruan stood.

At last she said, ''There it is! Look, José!''

I looked back, and in three places on the highest part of the Ruan walls, I could see fires burning.

''They give our direction, José!'' said the girl.

''We'll switch directions, then,'' said I, suddenly.

''It's no good trying,'' she answered. ''San Jacinto has to be our goal. There's no other, now that we've come this far. Otherwise, they'll have us running from point to point all night, and in the morning, they'll round us up like two poor cattle—and there's death for you in that, José, and something worse for me.''

I understood her perfectly well.

We reached the stream in the center of the valley, now, and Doloritas insisted that we should not go out of our way to ride to the nearest bridge, but that we should attempt to ford.

It was almost the end of both of us. The water was shallow

and the stream was not wide, but it leaped at us like running volleys of spears. When the current was no higher than the knees of the horses, it washed up in curling ripples as high as their bellies.

They staggered, and finally the roan, which was working upstream of the mule to break the force of the water a little, pitched his head under and was rapidly whirling down the current in a trice.

That should have been the end of both of us. For there were enough pointed rocks, a little farther down, to have eaten us like sharks' teeth.

But Doloritas saved us.

She had got her mule into the shallows, and uncoiling a rawhide rope from the pommel of her saddle—I had not noticed it there before—she threw it with an aim as good as that of any vaquero. She snared the head of the roan, and the pull the mule gave fetched us both into the safe shallows.

The roan was half choked, and I was more than half scared to death, but at least we were safe, though shuddering with something more than cold.

Doloritas did not seem in the least alarmed. She sat her mule on the top of the bank, calmly recoiling the rope, and laughing down at me, as I came up the bank on the roan, like a wet mouse on a wet rat.

Then we straightened our animals across country, and Doloritas pointed out to me the gap between the mountains which was the entrance to that gorge in which San Jacinto lay.

It looked very close, now. Not even the mist of the moon shrouded the mouth of it, which was guarded by two long, sloping hills, like couchant beasts, rudely cut from the rock. Like guardians they looked to me, I must say. For inside of them we ought to find our safety.

I said to Doloritas, as we allowed the animals to walk up a slope, "There's no danger, my dear. There's not a thing in view. There's not a sight to be seen. Everything's well with us, tonight!"

"José!" she cried back at me, impatiently, angrily: "Oh,

be a brave man and a wise man. Danger is sure to jump up in our path before long. It's not a common man we have to handle. It's El Blanco himself! El Blanco himself!''

I grunted a little, as the roan jolted into a canter again, downhill, but I was beginning to see that Doloritas, sweet and gentle and frail as she was, nevertheless, had a will of her own, and that after she was my wife, she might make things hum for me, now and then.

Well, what could be better for me than a strong-minded helpmate? What could be better? Nothing that I could think of. Certainly I had drifted in a most foolish fashion about this world up to the present moment. Now I would do better. And Doloritas would be my panacea.

We were getting forward at a good pace. We were coming on toward the mountains at such a rate that they seemed to break up, separate, and all flow toward us, growing huger and huger, with the moon striking brilliancies from the rocks, making them seem metal, and the forests as dark as plumes.

So we entered the San Jacinto gorge, and saw the two long, sloping hills that guarded the entrance slide past us upon either hand. And I heaved a great breath of relief. For I felt that we were through the gate of safety.

But Doloritas, it was plain, was not relaxing. She rode crouched in her saddle like a jockey—or a cat. And ever and again her head was turning as she looked for danger about her.

Yet nothing appeared. We had seen no living thing in all our way from the house of Ruan, and now the only noticeable sound about us was the groaning of the tired mule, and the snorting of the roan to clear its nostrils.

The thunder struck from that clear sky.

I saw the mule stumble, lurch forward, and then continue lurching, with its body falling faster than its weary feet could take up the ground. It struck heavily. It rolled head over heels, and lay still. Doloritas was hurled from the saddle and struck through a patch of brush ahead, and rolled from there onto the ground.

I threw myself out of the saddle and ran to her, the rein of the mustang hooked over my arm, but she was already on her knees as I came up.

Behind us the rifles were clanging, and the bullets thumped the rocks about us, or went with a brittle rattling through the brush.

I caught up Doloritas and swung her with one effort into the saddle of the roan. I had given one look to the mule and knew by that glance that it would never rise again.

"Go on!" I told her. "Go fast. I'll check 'em here if I can. Get help from San Jacinto and rush them back—hurry, Doloritas—"

"To leave you—" she cried.

"For heaven's sake, or we're both gone!" I begged.

She looked behind. She saw the rush of the dark riders, and with no other word she bowed her head and flogged the roan into a full gallop.

· 14 ·

WELL, IMPULSE JUMPS US INTO STRANGE SITUATIONS, BUT never was there one stranger than this of mine.

I turned about, and I saw that by a mere gesture, so to speak, I had placed myself in the boots of a hero. They were much too large for me. I saw that at once, but there I was, standing in them. And the terrible, bold bright moon was glaring in my face, and through the moonshine, lunging up the narrow of the gorge, was that evil flight of riders charging me.

At least, I had sense enough to see that I had no time to run either to the right or the left, and hide among the rocks. So, with my back to the wall, I lifted my rifle and tried to split that charge. I fired high, and I fired low, and those plunging, lunging fiends in full flight made no answer but seemed to hold their fire, in contempt, and ready to blast me from the face of the earth. For I could see the gleam of their weapons, held ready, and I could even make out some of the savage faces.

I felt that I was already dead. I stood with my finger crooked about the trigger unable to fire a third time, because I saw that there was no use in firing. Another instant and I would be riddled. I would be beaten shapeless under foot by the striding of half a dozen horses, and the same wave that destroyed me would wash swiftly up the valley and over-whelm poor Doloritas. This would be her last flight. Now in one instant, under the very walls of San Jacinto, as it were, he would sweep her up.

Some one in the cavalry charge was laughing in a wild, triumphant voice, and I swore that that was the man.

But now, when the forefront of the wave was looming over me, as it were, I heard a voice that shrilled and squeaked above the uproar and that screeched, in perfectly familiar English accents. "Don't fire! Don't fire! It's Joe!"

Why, it was the voice of the boy, the voice of Chip, con-found him! It was that same little scoundrel whose machi-nations—for what reason I could not guess—had brought me all this distance to the southland, and plunged me into this very pit where I stood.

In answer to that screech came a deeper, a roaring voice of command, in Spanish, and it was something to the effect that he would brain the fellow who harmed a hair of me.

Ah, well, there you are.

I should have died that instant, but the cry of Chip was the insect's sting that numbed the hand about to strike me, and the roaring voice of command turned that charge better than a shower of bullets could have done, so that all in a trice they had swirled away to this side, and to that, and they were sheltered among the rocks, while I, a single man, stood out there in the naked open space of the sandy bottom of the little gorge, held up as in the palm of a hand to the full silver stream of the moonlight!

Why, I was dead, and again dead, and a thousand times dead, if they chose to do the killing!

And the barking voice of Chip squeaked and rattled at me, "Joe, Joe! Get out of the way! Throw your rifle down, or you're a goner—"

I did not throw the rifle down. I was too stunned to react in time and stood there stunned, a fool, with the gun still in my hand.

"Let me shoot the gringo dog, señor! Let me shoot him,

El Blanco!'' I heard a Mexican screaming, in a fury of hatred and of battle-lust.

But the same ringing voice which had commanded before now said, "It's too late. She's right under the gate of San Jacinto, now! She's saved!'' He added, lowering his voice a little, "Joe, will you make a truce, confound you?''

And out into the moonshine, without waiting for my answer, stepped the leader, the celebrated El Blanco, the man-slayer, the wild cat who jumped the wall of a city at a bound. And I saw before me none other than Dug Waters—White Waters we used to call him—sauntering straight toward me, with one hand resting lightly on his hip.

My amazement made the gun slide out of my loosened grasp.

"Dug Waters!'' I gasped at him. "Dug Waters, of all men!''

"You've gone and turned yourself into a hero, since I last saw you, Joe,'' says he, very calmly, but with bitterness enough in his voice.

"You!'' I gasped at him, still more than half overcome. "You! El Blanco?''

"Yeah,'' said he, drawling as always. "El Blanco is what they call me in this neck of the woods. But, white or black, always the same, and your friend, Joe, since the night you helped to pry me out of the jail, and out of the hangman's noose!''

He came close up to me and held out his hand. I took it, and I wrung it, I was so glad to see him again. Particularly at that moment.

"How could you help doing it, Dug?'' said I. "How could you help blowing me to blasts out of your way, when I—''

I finished by pointing up the gorge, and as I pointed, deeply booming and welling down the valley I heard the clangor of the alarm bell of old San Jacinto there behind us. It was like an answer to my gesture. It was a weird, a sudden, and an awful thing at that moment, as though the mountains were giving utterance.

That sound, mind you, was dull with distance, but the

hideous clangor of it, the crowding, multiplying, echoing and reechoing notes put a madness in the mind.

"Well, Joe," said Waters, "I'm one of those simple fools who learn one thing at a time, and not many of those things; and, first of all, I learned always to stick to a partner. Which you were to me, one day, and which I therefore am to you forever! She's gone out of my hands, now, and forever, I suppose! But I couldn't blast the rock out of the way, not if the rock were your face, old-timer!"

His men were coming out from the rocks with their horses, now. And a more savage crew I never saw in all my born days. They came up to me exactly as cats would come up to a bird. In spite of Dug Waters as a friend. I was frightened still.

"Only," said Dug Waters, "I'd like to know what made you do it? What brought you so far just for the sake of downing me, old son?"

"Downing you?" said I. "I have here wrapped up inside of my shirt what brought me all of the way to this place. I never thought about you, at all!"

"Just what brought you, then?" said he.

I took out the ivory plaque which I had had from Chip, and I unwrapped the silk that hulled it about and bared the face to Waters, as reverently as a mother bares the face of its sleeping child to a stranger.

He saw it, and then he started with a grunt. He whirled on his heel, calling out, "Chip! Come here!"

For an answer, there was a glimpse of the boy bounding onto the back of a mustang and then scurrying down the gorge.

"Catch him, some of you!" shouted Waters. "Take my horse, Pedro. Catch him, and bring him back the way a bird dog brings a bird. If you hurt him, I'll cut your throat. If you get him, I'll give you ten dollars!"

I think every man of them shot into saddle to try to win the glory and the cash reward for that service. Off they went like a roll of thunder that walks halfway down the arch of the sky while you count three.

And before we could much more than count ten, they stopped the chase and started back for us, with the boy tethered and held fast among them.

He was dragged up before the chief, and then he was flung down to the ground just where we stood. It was that same Pedro who had been favored with the horse of his chief who had achieved the reward. He was the most beautiful villain I ever have seen. A great streak glistened like a mark of oil across half of his face. It was the sign of a frightful knife-cut in some brawl. He smiled, and it was like the horrible, brainless laugh of a fool—the scar tissue so pulled and twisted the face.

"Thank you, señor," said he, as he took the money. "I would as soon have done it for nothing, and I would rather have caught him with a rope than with my hands. I would rather have dragged him back at the end of the rope than carried him! You pay me for my own pleasure, señor."

I thought that Chip would twist himself in two, like the imp in the fairy story, he was so angry, when he heard this. He said, "You pie-faced, lantern-jawed, squint-eyed, half-nosed, raw-eared, halfwit! There never was a time when you could catch me, if somebody didn't give you a hoss too good for you. And there never was a time, after you caught me, that you could've handled me, if it hadn't been that you had a crowd with you. I'd meet you alone in day or dark, you skunk, and take off your hide in ten minutes by the clock, and you know it!"

This was a good deal to say to any one. And it was a great deal too much to speak to hot Mexican blood. That Pedro didn't stop to reflect. He simply pulled a gun and made a leap for Chip, and Chip looked to me halfway down the jaws of death.

He stood straight and still, facing the rush; but at the last instant he collapsed as quicksilver from a bag. He dropped in a lump right at the feet of Pedro.

It's a good trick, but one of the very hardest that any fighting man ever learned. Pedro was reaching for the throat of the lad with his long, moon-bladed knife, and just as he reached, his target disappeared and Pedro found himself stubbing his toe against a rock, as it were.

He tumbled head over heels, and landed with a grunt and a gasp, the wind flattened right out of him.

Young Chip, cool as you please, walks over and picks the knife out of the numbed fingers of the outlaw's hand.

"This has a pretty good point," says he, stepping back and trying the edge with his thumb. "You take my knife in exchange. It's good enough for the likes of you!"

With that, he outs with his own hunting knife, and throws it straight through the throat of Pedro. No, not through the throat, though it seemed so at first, but right into the hard-packed sand at the side of Pedro's neck. The cold of the side of the knife-blade sent a shiver through the whole body of Pedro!

The Mexican got up with a howl, and I think that he would have charged Chip again, but the chief stopped him with a word.

"You've got ten dollars and you've exchanged your knife, that's all," said he. "If you try that again, Chip will cut your throat for you, and if he doesn't—then I will."

· 15 ·

THIS FLURRY SEEMS NOT SO MUCH IN THE TELLING, BUT IT made my wits spin to see it. It showed me the hand and heart of that mob of tigers, as it were. And I wondered at a fellow like Dug Waters, who could live among these fellows and rule them so easily. He seemed perfectly at his ease, but the look that Pedro gave him, after receiving the rebuff, would have kept me awake for a month.

Now the attention turned back to Chip.

Said Waters, "Tell me, you little miserable sneak-thief, chicken-lifter, and gunfighter, you worthless thug and train-wrecker, you—tell me what became of the picture that I used to own? The picture of Doloritas, I mean?"

"Why," said Chip, "you long-drawn-out son of a north wind and a black night, why the deuce should I talk to you, anyways?"

Waters took him by the collar.

Chip answered with a neat wrestling hold that shook and almost tumbled Waters—but not quite. It was a strain and a tug, but he mastered Chip, and held him with an arm twisted behind his back.

Chip snapped over his shoulder like a dog biting at flies,

"The next time, or pretty near the next, I'll put you down, Dug, you skinny, four-flusher."

"The next time, I'll break your back for you," says Dug Waters.

He was hot and half meant it. But I knew that this pair loved one another. They had proved it a thousand times.

"Now," says Dug, "will you answer me what I'm asking you?"

"Not if you break my arm out of the joint," says the kid, through his teeth.

At that, Dug turned him loose.

I was amazed. The boy turned around, rubbing the shoulder which had been twisted, and Dug moved slowly away, with his back turned to him, thoughtfully scuffing at the sand.

"Hey!" says Chip.

"Well, partner?" says Dug, and stops, but doesn't turn around.

"Am I still that?" asked the kid, with a shake in his voice.

"Ay, always that—in spite of men!" said Dug.

"Or women?" asks the boy.

Dug waited a moment. I could see the black fiend in his face coming and going. But then he said, "All right. In spite of that, too."

Chip came up and went around and faced Waters.

"Look at me, Dug," says he.

"Yeah, I'm looking at you," says Dug, staring down at the ground, instead.

Chip drags in a deep breath. "What I mean to say is this," said he. "I swiped the thing, but I done it for you."

"You swiped it from me—for me?" asks Waters.

"That's it."

"You be the teacher and explain," says Waters. "It's pretty hard for me to follow that kind of algebra."

"All right. I'll try to explain," says the boy. "You're gonna hate me, Dug."

"Maybe not," says Waters.

But he was holding himself hard. That was plain to see.

"But I'll come clean," says the kid, shuddering as he says it.

"All right. You come clean, then," says Waters.

"And then?" says the kid.

"Then we can shake hands—and say good-by," says Waters.

It froze Chip. It turned him to stone. His round face was marble white, with the moon shining against it.

But he half whispered, "Yeah. I'll come clean, and take my licking. I'll tell you what, Dug."

"What?" says Waters.

"I seen that it wouldn't do."

"What wouldn't do?"

"These here international marriages."

"What are you talking about, Chip."

"I mean, suppose that you hook up with Doloritas—blast her!—it ain't any good. It don't pan out. It don't work. It never does work none. I've seen it plenty, too. You take 'em by themselves, and the Mexicans are all right. They're fine. I don't say nothing agin' them. Only, you see how it is? I've watched twenty of 'em get married to Americans, and most generally it's a bust. They got different ideas. They're raised different. It don't work out hardly never. I been told so, and I seen so, too! D'you foller that drift?"

Waters took out a bandanna from his pocket and mopped his forehead. He still was holding himself pretty hard, and he was perspiring.

"Well, I'm trying to foller along," says he.

"Well, Dug," says the boy, making his points with a fore-finger in the palm of his hand, "it's like this—you see Doloritas, and she knocks you off your horse. Ain't that right?"

"That's right enough," says Dug Waters.

"She knocks you off your horse," goes on the kid, "and you land on your ear and you see stars, and you think that she's one of 'em. Am I wrong?"

"Go on," says Waters.

"What's gunna be done about it? Nothin'! Old Ruan, he wants her married, but not to your kind. Anything else will do for him, because you've given him a bad raiding before. Ain't that right?''

"Yes, that's right.''

"And if anybody else comes along, you'll give him a slug of lead for a present to help him along in his courting. Ain't that right?''

"Yes, that's right too,'' admitted Waters. "Go on, kid.''

"I'm making it all straight,'' says the boy. "It's like this way. I say to myself: if Ruan won't let the chief have her, and if the chief won't let anybody else have her, there's just gunna be general heck poppin' all the while. And pretty soon there's a grand bust, and nobody gets any good out of it. And so what's to be done?''

"Go on,'' says Waters, through his teeth.

"So I says to myself,'' went on the kid, "that there's only one thing to happen, and that's to get Doloritas married off—not to Dug, but to somebody else that Dug can't handle.''

"Like whom?'' says Dug.

"Like a friend of yours,'' says the boy, "because I know that you'll never put hand on a friend of yours. I know that a friend of yours may stop bein' a friend, but that he's always sacred to you.''

"By Hector, I begin to see!'' says Dug.

"So I slide away, that time—you remember when I was gone three weeks?''

"Yeah, I remember,'' says Dug, gritting his teeth.

I begin to feel a considerable chill, for my part, when I saw how the thing was shaping up. I began to see my own part coming into the headlines, so to speak.

"Well,'' went on the kid, "all the time I'd been thinking. How many friends did you have in the world. They ain't so thick.''

"No,'' reflected Dug Waters. "I can step around between them without crowding myself none.''

"Then I remembered,'' said the kid.

"You remembered what?''

"I remembered about old Joe, my partner, that had helped in the party when you were pried out of jail. I knew that you'd never forget what he'd done, because what he done, he had nothing to gain by it. You were nothing to him. It was just out of the heart that he done it.''

"By thunder!" said Waters, and stared hard at me.

"That was why," said the boy, his voice getting tense again. "That was the whole reason. Will you believe it?"

"Go on! Go on!" said Dug Waters.

"So I thought that I'd get him interested in the girl. And so I swiped your picture of her on the ivory. And so I rode away and I found him and I showed it to him. And he come along down here on a string. If you know what I mean!"

"Ay," said Waters, slowly and bitterly. "That's a string that would pull a whole fleet along."

"And down he came, and right away quick," said the kid, "he gets to work and starts out like a real man, and he takes the girl away from the place, and then you come after and you're about to swaller him, when I sing out his name to you, and you stop, and so that's why we're standing here, and she's safe, up there in the town. Now you know everything. And I guess that it's good-by, partner."

Dug Waters, he takes a pace up and down and he thinks about the thing a little, and after a while he steps up to me, and he says, "Joe, what did you guess in this here job?"

I said, "I guessed nothing. I saw that picture, and I started the way that a horse starts when it smells oats!"

He laughed a little, with his teeth shut.

Did you ever hear a man laugh in that way? It's not so good to listen to!

Then he said, "I believe you. I believe everybody. But here I am, dang it, after making my play, and nothing to show for it, except ten dollars that I've spent to get this rat by the neck again!" He turned back sharp on the boy.

And poor Chip threw up his hands, as if to parry a punch. And then he dropped his hands and stood straight and still, like some one facing a firing squad. He stood there, marble under the moon, and he waited, and Waters stared at him, with a glimmer of bad fire in his eyes.

I tapped Dug on the shoulder. I tapped him pretty hard.

He whirled about on me, and I drew him one step away. I whispered in his ear.

"Waters," says I.

"Well?" says he.

"Ain't the kid worth about everything?" I said. "And who was he working for, and riding three weeks for? Himself?"

He gave a grunt, and that grunt was from the place where the stomach hurts the most when it aches. And he says to me, "Right, by gosh!"

He went back to the kid. He took him by both shoulders.

"Kid," he says, "I loved her."

"Ay," says the kid. "You're danged right that I knew that!"

"But," says Dug Waters, "I've had your life, and you've had mine, and there ain't any woman that can come between us. I can't say that I'll forget it, but I'll forgive it."

And they gripped their hands together.

· 16 ·

RIGHT HERE IT OUGHT TO BE REMEMBERED THAT CHIP WAS only sixteen, and that he'd been under a pretty big strain and had been facing the loss of a man that meant more to him than any one else in the universe. And Dug Waters, he begins to talk in a loud voice, and he orders everybody to their horses, and when he can't think of anything else to do, he coughs and hems and clears his throat, and I begin to curse at the dead mule, and kick at the sand, and act like a fool, generally, anything to make a loud noise—because I'd heard something like a whimper from the kid, and I knew that Chip was crying.

Well, we covered it up pretty well, and not a one of those Mexicans ever knew that Chip had acted, for a minute, like a plain ordinary boy.

He mastered himself pretty fast, and we all got to horse, and Dug Waters, he rides alongside of me and he says, "Look at here, son. This girl—what's she mean to you?"

"Everything," says I.

"Well," says he, "she doesn't mean everything to me."

"No," says I. "You've got a head on your shoulders. The kid means more to you."

"Yes," he says. "You're right that he does. But about this girl—you want her pretty bad?"

"I want her pretty bad," says I.

"And she wants you?"

"She asked me to run with her," I told him.

"Humph!" says he. "And she's a straight shooter?"

"Never none straighter, I guess," says I, slowly.

"Then you ought to have her," said he, grimly.

"I mean to," said I. "In spite of everything!"

He looked straight at me, and then he laughed a little. Well, I didn't mind the laughter very much. Because I saw what was in his mind. I wouldn't have had her, if Chip hadn't played my hand for me.

"Come on, Joe," said he. "I'm for the men, and not for the women. You're my friend, and I reckon that a friend is more to me than a wife ever would be. You wanta go to San Jacinto. So you come with me."

That was what we did. We rode up there through the gorge, with the moonshine glimmering and twinkling along the rocks, and a little creek came out of nowhere and began to sing at the feet of our horses, but we didn't stop to drink, or to let the horses drink. We just went out, and pretty soon, we came around a turn, and the valley widened a little, and there were the big, bulging, crumpling walls of dobe that surrounded San Jacinto.

It had been walled against Indians, in the first place. It was kept walled against the thugs, the cattle rustlers, and the gunmen of a later time; and still the people in that little place knew how to turn out when they heard the alarm bell begin to clang.

When we came out, about a dozen rifles clanged on the walls and sent wasps singing through the air.

We pulled back into the shadows of the gorge.

"Listen, Waters," said I. "They'll shoot at twenty, but they won't shoot at one. I'm going to ride in alone, and you'll see them open the gate for me!"

"I'm gunna wait," said he. "I dunno what I see. But if I see you dead, I'll hang twenty of them for the sake of you—or fifty, if you say the word."

"No," says I. "There's no chance. They won't shoot at a single man."

And they didn't.

I rode right in under the walls, up to the light that burned by the gate, and when I got there, I didn't have a chance to speak, for a voice sings out:

"Don José?"

"That's me," says I.

"You have come for the lady?" says the voice.

"I've come to see her," says I.

"You can see a letter from her," says the voice.

And right away, a letter was thrown down to me. I opened it. There was a touch of perfume in the paper. I held it to my face and breathed of it. I kissed that paper, in fact, because I was pretty far gone.

And this was what I read by the red light of the lantern at that gate, like the gate of an old castle of the Middle Ages:

DEAR JOSÉ: You have saved me, and you have lost me. From the first, I never wished for you. I wished for another man. He is here with me. He sits beside me, and watches me as I write these words. And he stops me, for he kisses the hand that writes them.

He is the man I love. I have waited these years for him. At last I have escaped my uncle, and I am with him. And I have escaped because of you.

What shall I say? That I am unfair? No, because whatever is done for love is not really unfair.

If you curse me, curse all women. For my sin is only their sin.

Dare I ask you to forgive me?

Well, remember the river, and the flow of the water, and the rope that saved you. And, remembering that, I dare ask you to forgive me.

And I wish to say, also, that I never would have dared, except for a word from the boy, because after he spoke to me, I knew that you were safe from El Blanco.

But you did not know. You thought that you were facing a foe, and not a friend.

If you read this letter it is because the boy was right, and El Blanco would not harm you.

In any case, Heaven be kind to you, Heaven reward you! From me, and from my husband, you have our love forever.

Is that enough?

Ah, my friend, remember that love is a fire that burns whoever touches it. I have touched it, and my brain is flaming. May yours, on a better day, burn for a better woman than for me.

Adios, with a thousand hopes for your happiness.

MARIA.

Well, I read that letter once, and I was stunned; and I read it again, and I was staggered; and I read it a third time. And then I leaned a hand against the wall of the town, and I laughed, and I laughed for a long time.

"Hai, señor!" says the voice of the man who had thrown me the letter.

"Hai, señor," says I. "Are you the man?"

"I'm the man," says he.

"Then put strong locks on your doors," says I.

"To keep out thieves?" says he.

"No, but to keep them in," says I.

So I rode back to the gorge. I was not very sick of heart. Because I had begun to see things that made me laugh. I felt, almost, as though I had thrown off a fur coat on a hot day.

In the shadows of the gorge, I found that the Mexicans had ridden on ahead. I could hear the jingling of their spurs, far off. Only Chip and Waters waited for me.

And so the three of us fell in, side by side, and we rode down the dimness of the valley, and not a word did we speak, and only the creaking of one saddle spoke to the creaking of another.

But I knew that a great thing had happened. For a woman had come, and a woman had gone, and she had made us three friends forever.

FORGOTTEN TREASURE

IN THE BEGINNING, EVERY QUINCE WAS FAIR OF HAIR; EVERY
Dikkon was dark. Every Quince was tall and broad; every
Dikkon was narrow and small. Every Quince had an eye of
green. Every Dikkon had an eye of black. And He who made
them so different set down the families side by side in the
mountains of Kentucky.

War, of course, followed; and though the Quinces were
bigger and wider and correspondingly stronger they simply
offered a fairer target to the guns of the Dikkons and, finally,
a scattered handful of the fair-haired giants packed their be-
longings and started for the Far West. On the way, a cruel
band of Dikkons swept down upon them and harried them so
dreadfully that, in the end, only two small families gained
their distant goal.

But even these were not left in peace, for Fate led the
Dikkons in numbers to the same spot, and the feud began
again. Finally the name of Quince was reduced to a single
man, and that man was outlawed. He married and left a son
behind him when five of the Dikkons cornered him in a nest
of rocks and paid three lives for his one.

It was considered that the price was small, for the more the
Quinces were reduced in number, the greater became their

strength. Now that this dangerous father was dead, it only remained to comb the mountains and find the boy who lurked somewhere among them. He was but twelve years old and, therefore, when he was found, the last of the viper breed would be wiped out. So they searched for young Barney Quince; twice they found his bullets, but him they did not find.

He eluded them, and again and again he dodged their searchers. However, the game became so hot that he was forced to leave that district. For three years he disappeared from the Dikkon ken, and their tribe increased and flourished. They nearly owned the rich town of Adare with all the valleys for farming and the highlands for grazing which lay around it. The Dikkons, and those who had married into the clan, owned this region; and they dominated the country, elected the officials, and above all saw that the dignity of sheriff should be vested in a person of the right Dikkon lineage.

Then Barney Quince came back in his sixteenth year and fell upon them like a plague. Their champions rode out against him and came back with weary horses and some empty saddles, but Barney they could not get. They might cut him with their bullets, but they could not cut him to the life-spot!

All that the Dikkons had he looked upon as his perquisite. If he needed money, it was a Dikkon whom he robbed. If he was lacking a swift horse, it was from the Dikkon herds that he cut out the best and the strongest. If he wished for meat, a Dikkon beef or a Dikkon mutton was his victim. And all of this he did with the price mounting upon his head, but his heart free from the sense of guilt. For, it was apparent, he had been nurtured deep in the lore of the Quince family. His mother had lived long enough to teach him all the past, poisoned with her bitter tongue. So he preyed upon the Dikkons with the subtlety of a desperado and the boldness of an honest man. His known boast was that never a man had fallen before him except one who bore the name of Dikkon, and never a penny of money had been taken at gunpoint except money made by a Dikkon; and never a morsel of food passed his lips except what he robbed from the Dikkons. To labor on his own behalf he scorned, and he swore that all that fed and clothed him should be reaped from the possessions of his hereditary foes.

So for ten dreadful years he was a scourge upon the backs of his foes, and they hushed their children at night with his name, and every young Dikkon grew into manhood with a single glorious goal before him—to find and destroy Barney Quince!

One question was asked repeatedly by the clan: had Barney Quince married? No, not yet! Therefore, there was no son and heir to his name and his terrors. The Dikkons might not capture him, but at least they drove him here and there like a swiftly glancing shuttle through the mountains and the valleys so that he could not mate. If they could not take him with their net, at least the peril would perish with him.

Yet others said that he knew this well and would choose his own good time to marry, and before he died surely another of his name would be riding and destroying as he had ridden and destroyed.

This was not merely an occasional theme with the Dikkons, but it mingled bitterly with the bread of every meal that was eaten in the town of Adare, and the sun never rose upon their rich valleys, their standing crops, their flocks and their herds without bringing the cold thought of Barney Quince.

Consider, then, what horror, wonder, joy, and disbelief were mingled in the souls of the clansmen when, as they sat at their supper tables one evening with the rose of the sunset time beyond their windows, they heard a startled rumor that Barney Quince had come down into the town itself!

They rushed out, all the men; the women and the children cowered behind; but the armed men, resolute and stern—for when was a Dikkon a coward?—formed a solid van with rifles ready, and then they saw the strangest sight that ever dawned upon their eyes.

For a tall man was walking lightly down the central street along which their houses faced, and behind him stepped a magnificent horse, a gray that glimmered brightly in the rose of the evening. They knew the horse and they knew the man.

When it was a magnificent three-year-old, the hope and the pride of the heart of Harvey Dikkon, the colt had been stolen from him by the marauder, and for three years now it had served to whisk the evildoer away from his pursuers. That was the gray; and walking before him was Barney Quince, with his long, yellow hair shining as it had shone many a time before, blinding the eyes of the Dikkon clansmen. But at the back of his head it was stained and clotted with blood! And that blood, and his gay and careless manner as he descended into the town of his enemies, made his coming something that chilled their very souls, because it was a ghostly thing, beyond human understanding.

It was doubtless this sense of the unearthly that had caused many a rifle, raised to cover him, to fall slowly again, while the gunmen gaped and shook their heads; but when he came to the very center of the village, old Ned Dikkon, with a cry, started out into the roadway and brought his rifle to his shoulder.

There was no doubt in his mind; and as for a sense of ghostliness in this proceeding, he was familiar with the sad touch of the other world, for his two strong sons had been taken from him, his two gallant boys who stood in the very forefront of the clan for the manliness and skill in all that makes a Western rider formidable and famous. They had been taken from him, and there came the man who had stopped their lives—both in one sudden battle of an August afternoon, where the trail turns on the gray shoulder of Mount Forrest.

He shouted: "Barney Quince, think of Pete and Charlie Dikkon that you murdered!" And he pressed his steady finger slowly around the trigger.

That bullet would have found the heart of Barney Quince, without doubt; but Oliver Dikkon, when he saw his older brother start out, rifle in hand, ran after him, and came in time to thrust the weapon aside and then wrest it from his grasp.

"Man, man!" he called. "You wouldn't do a murder?"

That broke the spell. A flood of excited men bound the hands of Barney Quince—those terrible hands which now submitted passively—and they led him into the nearest house, which, by chance, was the house of Oliver Dikkon.

It was an excited crowd, and savage voices began to rise in it after the first shock of the surprise had worn away. Oliver

Dikkon took control, not only because he was one of the head men in the clan, but because he now could exert a doubled authority as the owner of the house in which they were crowded. He called together the half-dozen recognized leaders of his people; and the rest, though sullenly and ill at ease, departed from the dwelling and gathered in the front garden, overflowing into the street.

They did not leave, but remained there leaning on their guns. Behind them came the children swarming, and anxious mothers after them, telling them in shrill voices to come home again; for where Barney Quince was, there was peril! It was hopeless to try to convince them, however. They swarmed out as they would have swarmed to see the Giant whom Jack killed in the story, filled with fear, but also filled with expectant delight.

In the meantime, the grim voices among the men were raised now and again. There was not one among them who had not had a father, a brother, a son, a cousin destroyed either by this man or by his hardly less terrible father. There were none who had not ridden, at once time or another, upon his trail; there were many who were scarred by his bullets. There was gigantic Ben Dikkon, for instance, who had closed with the outlaw in single combat on one heroic and never-to-be-forgotten day when he had been left for dead. Now the scars of that dreadful fight were on his body and seamed his face; he towered above the rest of the smaller, dark-faced clansmen, and he alone said nothing, but his set jaw and his narrowed eyes told none the less plainly what stirred in his mind.

The others looked at him. Having met the destroyer and lived to tell the tale, he seemed to them like some primeval force, greater than other men, half godlike. They would have welcomed speech from him, but speech there was none. So silence gradually settled over the entire assemblage; even the children were quiet. Anxious eyes looked up and noted that clouds were gathering heavily across the face of the sun, and a wind cold as night blew down from the upper mountains. Some great event, they knew, was about to come to pass, and gloomily they felt that it boded not all good for the clan of Dikkon.

· 2 ·

WITHIN THE HOUSE THEY SAT IN A DULY ORDERED SEMI-circle. At its right tip was Randolph Dikkon, whose beard had been white for twenty years; next to him, Eustace, who was almost as old but who instead of turning white had remained gray and instead of withering had merely shrunk a little and grown harder and harder; little Henry Dikkon, on Eustace's left, owned a farm in Windale Valley and was prosperous enough for that alone to account for his place on the governing committee; John, beside Henry, had been educated in an Eastern university, and, growing soft in professional life as a lawyer, he alone graced Adare with a frock coat and a gold chain looped across his increasing stomach. Oliver had his place in this high body, well-earned whether as a fighting man, or a shrewd councilor, or as the proprietor of the lumber mill which, on the river just above the town, harnessed the stream and made it do his bidding. Last of all was Martin Glanvil, who had married into the clan and who was the first of a foreign name ever to sit in this august assemblage; and, therefore, despite his advanced years, he had the seat farthest left from the acknowledged master of the Dikkons. He was looked upon, to a degree, as an interloper, but the strength of his broad and patient mind had been tested often, and never had he been found wanting.

So the six wise men sat together and focused their grim attention upon the last of their hereditary enemies, he who alone stood between them and a permanent peace, now helpless in their hands. A cloth was tied around Quince's head, for Louise, Oliver's daughter and the woman of the house, had washed away the blood and found a ghastly wound in the skull; this she had dressed and now she stood observant close to the fire which burned on the broad hearth.

"He's had his head broken by a fall," she told them, "and his wits are gone! If you do anything to him, you've done something worse than the murder of a baby!"

Eustace Dikkon parted his hard lips.

"I remember the story of how the Quinces came down on the house of Jerry Dikkon in Kentucky and murdered the men, and locked the doors, and let the women and the children burn. There was a couple of babies inside, I've heard tell!"

And he explained his thin, flinty hands toward the distant blaze and rubbed them slowly together; but warmth he never would get into his flesh or into his heart.

"What's been done before by man or woman against the Dikkons ain't of account here and now," pronounced Randolph, his hand buried in his beard; "but only what's been done by this here man before us. Barney Quince, you stand up and answer what's asked of you!"

The prisoner, when he heard his name, looked up with a pleasant smile which made his handsome face actually beautiful, for an instant. But then the light went out of his face and he remained for a moment with lifted eyes, staring past the heads of the circle and into some vast distance.

"You see!" said Lou Dikkon. "He don't know a thing. You'd better put him to bed—and hang him when he gets his senses back!"

"Woman," said Randolph, "Leave the room!"

She could not argue against such resistless authority, but

for an instant she lingered beside the prisoner, and dropped her hand upon his great shoulder.

"He's done his killings," said she, "but he's never fought foul; he's never shot from behind; he's never been a snake in the dark. Dad, you won't let 'em murder this poor halfwit?"

Thunderous silence greeted this appeal, and she shrank from the room, only pausing at the door to cast back a single earnest glance at the big man who sat before the fire, with its light glimmering through his long golden hair and touching on the sea green of his eyes.

Still the silence held.

The hard lips of Eustace parted again. "Out on my place," said he coldly, "I halter-break the fillies as well as the colts!"

Oliver colored under his rebuke, but he made no answer. Old Randolph brought the talk back to its proper subject.

"I've called on you to stand up here, Barney Quince. You hear me talk?"

There was no reply. Barney Quince yawned broadly, touched the back of his head as though it had been stabbed by a pain, and almost instantly fell into deep study over a cricket which was crawling across the floor toward the heat of the fire.

At this, Randolph said: "He don't answer. "What's to be done?"

John Dikkon felt the eyes of the others turning toward him. He expanded a little. One hand he hooked in his massive golden chain. The other hand he laid upon his smooth knee. He depressed his chin a little and said: "In such a case, one might proceed by considering silence an affirmation. Threaten him, therefore, that you will proceed in that manner."

"John," said the chairman, "I reckon that you know what this Barney Quince is said to have done. You open up and ask him, all lawlike, if you please."

John stood up at once. He took a position in front of the captive and, thrusting one hand behind his back, he made the tail of his frock coat stand out like the tail of a rooster; then, leaning a little, he waved a fat forefinger like a club above the bent head of Barney Quince.

"You, Barney Quince," said the lawyer, "standing before this bar for judgment, and in your contumacy refusing to answer the questions justly put to you, being subject, justly, to its authority, are hereby declared to have returned an affirmative answer to those questions to which you return no answer except silence. Hear me, and reply if you have anything to say against this judgment."

The captive, during the latter part of this little oration, had listened to the speech with a sort of mild wonder, raising his head and regarding the orator with a wandering attention; but now he chuckled softly and, leaning forward, he picked up the cricket and placed it farther from the fire and in the long hair of a bearskin rug—a skin which Oliver Dikkon himself had brought home after a desperate battle with the original wearer.

John Dikkon turned and bowed to the reverend head of the court.

"The prisoner returns no answer, and thereby accepts the condition," he declared. "Shall I proceed with the examination?"

"D'you know what you're talkin' about, John?" asked Old Randolph.

"Sir," said the lawyer, "you forget that I am a Dikkon; no man is more familiar with the outrages which are attached to the name of this man."

"Go on, then."

The lawyer returned to the charge. Again his fat forefinger impended in the air.

"At the tender age of twelve years," said he, "an age when most men are children and unacquainted with the dreadful profession of arms, did you not, when three honorable gentlemen of the name of Dikkon were riding though the mountains, willfully assault them with intent to kill, actually shooting one horse from beneath the person of William Dikkon and striking Harry Dikkon through the shoulder, so that from that day until his death he never had proper use of the afflicted limb?"

"Go on," said Randolph, "you got a good memory, John,

but just leave out the age of him when you talk about what he's done to us!''

There was an affirmative stir in the court; Barney Quince was still rapt in the cricket.

"The prisoner returns silence," said the lawyer, "and thereby admits the charge of willfully and feloniously assaulting the persons of three men, killing a horse and seriously wounding one man. A serious charge!" affirmed John Dikkon.

He went on: "Did not you, not three months later, in the middle of the night, when two men entered your room in a hostelry known as Larkin's Luck, at a crossroads between Elkhead and Lewis' Crossing, willfully and with malice aforethought, with intent to destroy and take the lives of those two men—did not you, Barney Quince, with a gun in either hand, attack them, shooting Gerald Dikkon through the hip and the neck, so that he lay for months near to death; and did you not at the same time shoot Lawrence Dikkon through the head and through the body so that he did instantly fall down dead in that room? Answer, on the peril of your life''

The prisoner did not stir, and something between a groan and a growl was heard from the six judges.

"The prisoner returns no answer, and by the agreement already entered into with him," said the man of law, "this silence is accepted as an acknowledgment of the willful assault upon and murder of Lawrence Dikkon, together with the willful and malicious attack upon and the vital wounding of Gerald Dikkon!"

He made a little pause, then continued: "Three years elapsed, and then on a December night, did you not, Barney Quince, descend from the mountains and raid the ranch of Rathbone Dikkon, taking from him forcibly and at the point of a gun two horses, as well as a whole pack of guns, ammunition, and food of various kinds, being all that was in the larder of the said Rathbone Dikkon? And when he with his two sons pursued you, did you not attack the three, and willfully and with malice aforethought, with intent to slay, fire upon them, wounding Rathbone Dikkon through the right arm, and taking the life of Jerome Dikkon, his eldest son?''

He turned to the court.

"The prisoner remains silent," said the lawyer, "and thereby he pleads guilty to the second charge of having taken the life of a good and law-abiding American citizen, by name Jerome Dikkon, who had acted merely in defense of his just and legal rights!"

He made another pause, and was raising his fateful right hand once more for fresh accusation, when the sharp and brisk voice of Henry Dikkon broke in: "I dunno that there's any use asking the rest of the list, unless you can hang a man higher for fifteen murders than you can for two! Suppose that we start figuring what we're gonna do with this gent?"

The mention of the round number of actual deaths among the clan which had occurred because of this man caused a shudder to pass through the circle; but then there was silence, and all heads turned to Randolph Dikkon for his judgment.

• 3 •

Hᴇ ᴏꜰ ᴛʜᴇ ʟᴏɴɢ ᴡʜɪᴛᴇ ʙᴇᴀʀᴅ ᴄᴏᴍʙᴇᴅ ɪᴛ ꜰᴏʀ ᴀ ᴍᴏᴍᴇɴᴛ, intently eyeing the prisoner, and the latter, as though wearied of the cricket, now stood up and raised above his head his roped hands. He stretched, rising in tiptoe, and the ropes that bound his hands together creaked mightily.

At that, six guns appeared swiftly from beneath six coats, but the ropes held and the prisoner's hands fell before him once more.

"I guess I'd better be going," said he.

Oliver Dikkon met him and caught his arm.

"You sit down where you were," said he, sternly.

The big man looked down on the other, but without malice, and nodding his head cheerfully, answered: "All right, if that's what you want!"

He sat down; he searched with sudden care for the cricket, found it, and replaced it on the bear rug. Then he settled back to a more earnest contemplation of its peculiarities.

At last Randolph Dikkon spoke.

"We've got our man at last," said he, "and John says that he's admitted what we all know that he's done. I dunno what more we could ask for, and I guess that we got trees high enough to do what we want of them. Eustace, you'd better take charge of him, and the quicker that you get the thing over with, the better for him—and for us.''

Eustace rose, accordingly, with a slight hardening, if that were possible, of his features, and approached the prisoner.

"Stand up, Barney Quince!" he commanded.

The prisoner rose, and he smiled his beautiful smile at the little, frost-bitten Eustace.

At this, Oliver Dikkon started out of his chair and crossed to the pair. He tapped his elder cousin, Eustace, on the shoulder.

"Hold on a minute, Eustace," said he.

"You always was fond of talking, Oliver," said the older man. "But I dunno that talk will serve us now! There's a hanging to be got done with, Oliver!"

"I was just thinking—you're a man who's always handled dogs a good deal, Eustace!"

"And there's only one way to deal with a mad dog," said Eustace readily enough.

There was a deep throated murmur of assent, and Oliver nodded agreement.

"Certainly, you're right. But, tell me Eustace, when a puppy comes into your house and tears up a hat or a pair of riding boots, what do you do to it?"

"Thrash it, of course, and teach it better sense," said Eustace. "Stand out of my way, Oliver!" He said the last with a tone of anger, for Oliver Dikkon had interposed between him and the prisoner.

"I still have something to say," replied Oliver, "and I guess it's the rule with us that everybody has a chance to talk out what's in his head until Uncle Randolph overrules him. Is that right, sir?"

He of the white beard nodded gravely.

"Go on and talk, lad," he said. "I guess that nobody could improve on what you got sometimes to say! What's bothering you now?"

"I say," declared Oliver, "that there's no more difference between a grown dog and a puppy than there is between the

Barney Quince that killed our men, and the Barney Quince that's here in front of us now.''

This speech made a sensation, and hard-bitten Eustace said with a sneer, ''You kind of like this giant, Oliver. You kind of take to him, it seems to me!''

To this Oliver said sadly: ''I hope I've proved myself as good a Dikkon as you have, Eustace, though you're a good deal older than I am, and I suppose that you're wiser in most things. But I want to point out that nobody has lost much more than I have through this man. It was he that came down and burned my whole wheat crop and barn on my river farm, as any one can remember. And my two nephews that were raised about as much in my house as in their own—I mean poor Charlie and Peter—they both were killed by this man. I mean to say that I've got reasons both of hard cash and blood to hate him, and I think that I hate him as much as most of you do. But I got a couple of things to point out to you!''

There was a restless turning of heads to Randolph Dikkon, but since the old man said nothing, Martin Glanvil spoke up in his deep and growling voice: ''Facts is facts, and blood is blood. Unless they can be swallowed, this here man has got to die, Oliver!''

''Wait a minute,'' broke in Randolph Dikkon. ''We've got to hear everything that Oliver has to say, if he keeps us here all the night. Go on, Oliver!''

''Thanks,'' said Oliver. ''Then I'll talk up and say what I've got to say. I want to remind you of the time when Bud and Luke, Sam Dikkon's two boys, started out and swore that they'd never leave the trail until they'd found Quince. They found him, as you might remember. It was winter. They got to a shack and there they found the signs of Quince and they stayed there until the dark came down, and they lay quiet, ready to kill him when he opened the door.

''Well, he *did* open the door, at last, And they turned loose at him. He fell down in the snow with a bullet through his left leg, and lying there, he shot them both; and they surrendered to him wounded like he was, and they—''

"By heaven," cried Eustace, "I'm not gonna listen to this!"

"Steady! Steady!" said little Henry Dikkon. "We've got to take the bitter with the sweet."

"Then," went on Oliver, "he crawled in and took their guns. Bud was drilled right through the body, and Luke was shot through the shoulder, so bad that his arm ain't any good today. And Quince stayed there in the cabin with his game leg and helped to tie up their wounds, and for two months he kept them, and then he turned them loose, safe and sound, and let them ride down to the valleys again. And Bud and Luke, to this day, they never will say a word against him! Is that all a fact, or do I make it up?"

A gloomy silence answered this statement and appeal.

Finally the speaker went on: "Now, here we got Barney Quince. Did we go hunting for him? We did not! Did we get him by a fair fight? We did not! Did we buy him from his enemies, even? We did not! But he walked in and gave himself up, you might say, because he'd been hurt worse than through the body or the leg. He's gone in the brain, and there he is for any of you to see that he's got an empty brain. Now, men, I say that the killing of a man like that is worse than the murder of a baby, and I'll work and fight against it as long as I've got a thought in my head and a drop of blood in my body!"

"You think," said Eustace bitterly, "that because you stand in with him now, he'll stand in with you later on, when he's got better."

"How can he get better, once his wits have left him?" asked Oliver. "Look at him, will you? Studying a cricket while we try him for his life!"

"Maybe he's playing possum," suggested Glanvil sternly.

"And did that bring him down right into the middle of our town?" asked Oliver Dikkon.

"Speak up, Uncle Randolph," urged Eustace, in the greatest excitement, "and tell 'em that they're gonna bring down blood on their heads if they let this gent live!"

But Randolph Dikkon said not a word. Finally Henry broke

in: "I dunno how it is, but I got to agree with Oliver. That ain't a man, there. It used to be Barney Quince. It's the size and the shape of Barney Quince still, but it's just an empty shell, it seems to me. There's nothing inside of it, because a man with his wits gone is like a nut with the meat out of it. Killing Barney, here, you ain't killing the man that done the shooting of so many of our clan. It's like killing a stranger that never lifted a hand in his life to hurt nobody!"

This speech made two on the side of the prisoner, and all faces became grave.

John Dikkon burst out: "I say that I hate the face and the name of him, and no harm can be done by putting him out of the way. Let it be done legally, if you want. But let it be done. Bring him up for trial, then!"

"Bring him up for trial before Judge Postlethwaite," said Henry Dikkon, "and he'll send him to a home for the feeble-minded before the trial's a day old. Ask your own good sense, John, and you'll see that that's true!"

The lawyer was silenced, though he shook his head in a sullen denial that had no meaning.

"Uncle Randolph, will you give us a judgment, here?"

The old man sighed.

"There's no good going to come of it," said he, "but when two and two is put together, you got to say that it adds up to four, and the two and two that you name here, it looks to me that it adds up to what Oliver says. This man is no more than a baby, and the Dikkons never have loved the Quinces, but we never have been baby-killers. I guess that's about the end of things. Call Louise, Oliver, and ask her to get me a cup of coffee. I kind o' have a need for it before I go home in the cold."

Oliver went gladly to obey the order, but before he reached the door, Eustace whirled upon the others and raised a thin hand above his head. It was quivering with his wrath.

"I hear you talk, you gents," said he. "I hear you talk, and it's all very fine what you got to say. You talk about babies, and such. But I talk about Barney Quince, and I tell you that you'll never again have the chance that you've got now. Here he is that's done all of the murders, and if you let him go, you'll never have the like chance again. God forgive you all if you set him free to start on the trail again! More of us'll be hunted down. For the fifteen that he's killed already, a hundred is apt to drop before the finish; and, besides, he'll have the time and the chance to leave a son behind him to carry on for the name of Quince where he left off. I've got no part in this decision. I say that you're a parcel of fools. I'm going home, and I'll be damned if ever I come to another council of the Dikkons. Get another to take my place.''

• 4 •

THE HEAD OF BARNEY QUINCE HEALED IN DUE TIME, BUT never for an instant did it make him an invalid. He was constantly about the house of Oliver Dikkon, sometimes wandering into the fields, and sometimes climbing about the great lofts of the barn, where he seemed to take a peculiar pleasure in getting as far aloft as possible, and then sitting on a great crossbeam, or dizzily poised on the derrick rod which projected above the door of the mow, he would fall into broodings. Time seemed to him of no more moment than it is to a roosting owl. At night he slept in the hay; and often on the coldest nights he stretched himself on a mat in the kitchen, in front of the stove, but his long life in the wilderness had made the softness of a bed apparently distasteful to him.

He was not altogether simple, even though it seemed impossible for him to understand most of the words which were spoken to him. For instance, he allowed no tear to appear in his clothes without sitting down at once to mend it with a scrupulous fineness of handiwork which no woman could have surpassed. His skill at this suggested to Louise Dikkon other means of employing him so that he might be useful to the family which supported him now, and also to himself. For the doctor of the village of Adare could only suggest that constant occupation would be better for the poor, deranged, stunned mind.

Barney Quince was at the disposal of Lou Dikkon because, from the first day, he looked upon her with a great attachment—not as a man to a woman, but rather as a dog to a master. He would follow her about the house for hours; if she sat down to her sewing, he sat down crosslegged on the floor near by and seemed perfectly contented. If she went for a walk, he ranged with her, wandering with his rapid step here and there, sometimes running to a distance, but always circling back. Her father was alarmed by this constant attendance, but gradually every one came to understand that Barney Quince was utterly harmless.

So Louise began to employ this useless, mighty engine. She tried him at first at the woodpile, where the dried oak, hard as flint from the long seasoning it had received, had to be sawed into convenient lengths and then split. With her own hands she put the heavy and cumbersome crosscut in position and guided it for him. For the greater part of a day she worked at the lesson before he could learn what was wanted. Then he sawed through a segment readily enough, and as he grew warm with the work and rolled up his sleeves, she watched the sinewy muscles playing snakelike up and down his forearm. Then she understood why the giant who was the pride of Adare had been helpless in the hands of this warrior and she felt a great awe, such as may be felt by a trainer who compels lions to do trifling tricks.

It was very hard to make progress with him. When he had sawed through a log, he would come into the house bearing a ponderous section in his hands and offer it to her with a smile of childish joy; and she had to lead him back and replace the great saw at the proper point. It was a week before he could understand the whole business of wood-sawing, but after that he advanced into the huge pile of timber like a fire. When the sawing was done, she taught him to split the chunks to appropriate sizes, and then with much patience she instructed him in cording the wood in the shed. He seemed to feel no burden in these labors; and sometimes she would pause in her kitchen work, hearing out of the distance a great voice that swelled into a phrase or two of song. Only a little moment of music, and then a long silence, as though the fumbling brain had picked up a happy thread, only to lose it again almost at once.

After this start had been made with him, it was increasingly easy to teach him other tasks. She taught him to milk the string of cows and pour the milk into the pans in the creamery; and how to churn, and how to fork down the hay for the teams so that their mangers were filled when they came in from work at the plow. She even attempted to teach them to work the plow, but in this she failed utterly, for he persisted in leaving the team standing in the field, while he came back to the house to her. At any distance from her he was unhappy, bewildered, and through the day he had to come to her again and again and stand silently by, reading her face with an expression half intent and half wistful.

She became fascinated by her duties as schoolmistress and tried him at reading and writing, but here she had no success whatever; for though he might sit down and write off a whole sentence at dictation with a rapid and flowing hand, yet in the middle of a word the machine might stop and refuse to start again that day.

In the meantime, however, he had become a profitable worker, and Oliver Dikkon, estimating his value with a strict sense of honor, paid monthly wages into the hands of his daughter to be used for her protégé as she thought best.

Then she was seen walking down to the store, with the giant stepping softly behind her. And he stood by, vaguely pleased, while she bought clothes for him, and shoes.

There was one heart-stopping moment when he paused by the rack where the rifles stood and, taking out one of the best, opened the chamber and reached with an automatic hand for a cartridge, fumbling blindly when he discovered that he was not girt with the long-familiar belt.

However, he let her take the weapon from his hands and she led him away, past the pale-faced clerks.

She talked to her father about this incident, and he considered it for a long time before he made the most unexpected answer.

"You've got to let a man work along the lines that he knows," said Oliver Dikkon. "A fine cowpuncher may be a fool at books, and a bookman may be a fool with cows. A good miner might die of dry rot being a clerk; and so with Barney Quince that has lived by the gun for his whole life, pretty near—maybe one thing that keeps him back is not having a rifle, say! And plenty of chance to use it!"

"And—" she began.

"And if he should ever use it on a man—why, the man would be dead, and we'd have to kill Barney. It's a hard chance to take. But I think that there's no danger in him now. There's no meanness and there's no malice. I'm going to let you take him my best rifle tomorrow."

She was full of fear, but she recognized a sound reasoning behind this advice, and that same day she placed the rifle in the grip of Barney Quince and put on him the cartridge belt. For two days he was helpless with joy, sitting with the gun in his lap, admiring its brightness, patting it like a living creature. The third day he was found cleaning it; and the fourth day he disappeared!

Terror ran through the entire village of Adare. Swift messengers were sent to outlying workers in the fields. In dread and in silence they waited; but in the evening a giant walked from the shadows of the trees and strode across the fields carrying on his shoulders a deer which would have been well-nigh a burden for a horse. He kicked open the kitchen door, and laid it at the feet of Lou Dikkon. Then he stood by, panting with his vast labor, and laughing out of the joyous fullness of his heart.

All Adare breathed once more.

After that, there was hardly a day when he did not slip off from his other duties and hunt in the fields, in the woods, over the hills. He brought back rabbits; squirrels whose heads had been clipped off as though with a shears; deer; partridges; and the larder of Oliver Dikkon's place was crammed with fresh meat, and his neighbors came to bless the gun of

Barney Quince. It was at this period, also, as the spring
turned warm, that he was put on the trail of the lame grizzly
which for three seasons had devastated the valleys, choosing
with a nice taste the best of the yearling colts, dining once
upon each body, and then departing to come again.

For a week Barney Quince was gone and Eustace Dikkon
vowed that he never would be seen again. He was seen, however. With a great bearskin rolled on the back of a burro, he
trudged home to the house of Oliver Dikkon, and laid the
massive spoils before his mistress.

From that moment the attitude of Adare toward Barney
Quince altered perceptibly, for up to this time the villagers
had looked upon him as a public menace, a danger post-
poned, but inevitably sure to fall; but thereafter it was felt
that his old identity had been lost forever, and that he had
become a public benefactor. Moreover, they derived a rather
sinister satisfaction from the knowledge of what he had been,
and what he now was; and when they saw him striding down
the street behind his mistress, resolutely refusing to walk at
her side, they could not help smiling, one to another; for this
was as it should be, with a Quince! He was better than dead.
His old self had perished; he lived only to serve his enemies
like another Samson, with bonds not upon his body but on
his brain.

Lou Dikkon was aware of the public attitude; but her own
differed. She took great and greater care that he should not
be made an open show. When small boys formed the habit
of running after them, her father was sent to call on their
parents. Gradually people came to know that Oliver Dikkon
and his daughter respected this hulk which once had been so
great a ship, and, for the sake of Oliver Dikkon, the smiles
were ended.

So the bright heat of summer came to Adare, and with it
came the usual thin drift of Easterners, arriving for a vacation
among the mountains. Most important of these holiday-
makers was that great and good man, Doctor Mansfeld, from
New York.

On the very first day of his arrival he passed on the street the smiling face and the blank eye of the giant, and he stopped short and turned to look after him. Of course he had already heard the story. And that night, he came to the house of Oliver Dikkon and asked to see this stricken man.

He found Lou Dikkon at the piano, drawing accompaniments out of its untuned strings, while she sang like a bird; and, leaning on the piano, stood Barney Quince. He took no more notice of the doctor than a figure of mist. He allowed his head to be examined with perfect indifference; and afterwards, when Lou went to bed, he went after her, to lie in the hallway across her door.

The doctor remained behind with Oliver Dikkon.

· 5 ·

THE DOCTOR WENT STRAIGHT TO THE POINT.

It needed no special skill, he declared, to tell what was wrong with Barney Quince. It was the fall which had stunned him, of course, that had made him a halfwit, or something little better. And the reason he remained in that condition was simply that a segment of skull had been permanently depressed and bore down upon the brain. Now, there was one chance in ten that an operation would kill the patient; there were four chances in ten that the operation would do him no good; there were five chances in ten that he would be completely cured and made as intelligent a man as ever he had been before.

Oliver Dikkon listened; growing more and more tense, and his brown face lengthened with gravity.

Finally he said, "Suppose you win with him, Doctor Mansfeld. Then what'll he be?"

"An intelligent, alert man, once more."

"D'you know what kind of a man he was?"

"I've heard that he was a rough character, but his experiences recently, no doubt, will have tamed him. You have been kind to him, Mr. Dikkon. That kindness can't be forgotten."

Oliver Dikkon mused: "When he got the blow on the head, it wiped his memory clean. Lift the bone and probably he'll go back to the time when he had the fall. Ain't that possible?"

"It is," agreed the doctor unhappily.

"Fifteen men have been killed by Barney Quince," said Dikkon. "They were all my kin. Ten of 'em lived in Adare. I say that if you bring him back to his wits, so's he'll remember his own name, then he has to stand trial for fifteen killings, and the trial will be before a jury of Dikkons, and there ain't any doubt of what the verdict would be! You'd only be saving him to hang him, doctor! And if he didn't hang but got away, there's many a strong and brave man alive today that'll die under the guns of Barney Quince before he's ended with a bullet through his head."

All of this the doctor considered, and he could see the strength in the argument; yet he was pushed on by earnest devotion to his art. He argued: "Quince is already dead, and this poor creature who fills his body is neither man nor beast!"

"He's a man!" insisted Dikkon. "He does a man's work, too, and he's worth his pay. I'd rather have him the way he is, than any other two men on my ranch! What more d'you ask for him? He's happy. He loves my daughter. She can make him do anything. She's teaching him a little more and more all the time. Maybe he'll wake up entire, one of these days, except that he won't know he's Barney Quince, and born and raised to kill me and my family. Ain't there a chance—that he'll get pretty normal, I mean?"

"There is no more chance of that," said the doctor, "than there is that he'll walk to the moon! I leave this matter on your conscience, Mr. Dikkon; but if I were in your place, I should not like to have on my mind that I've stood between this man and his true self!" With that, he left.

Two days later Dikkon came to the hotel where Mansfeld was putting the finishing touches to his preparations for the mountains.

"I've talked it over with my daughter," said he. "I didn't

call in the older heads of my people, because I knew before-hand what they'd say. I've talked it over with my daughter, and she's been driving me on to it. If you say the word, she'll bring Quince in to you whenever you wish."

So that matter was arranged, and the doctor hurried on his work, arranged for a room that would serve for the operation, found by keenest good luck a skilled assistant, and prepared his instruments.

Early the next morning, Lou Dikkon came to the hotel, and behind her walked Barney Quince. She stood in front of great Doctor Mansfeld and said to him, all pale and still of eye: "If ever Barney Quince kills another man, doctor, what will you think about it?"

The doctor did not like this view of the matter. He said something about the necessity for serving the will of Nature with the skill of science. But he was so ill at ease that he rushed on the preparations, and soon Barney Quince was alone with the doctor, his assistant, and half a dozen strong fellows who were to help during the anesthetizing process.

That process had hardly begun before there was a violent disturbance in the operating room; wild cries were heard; the door was split clean in two, from top to bottom, and Barney Quince rushed out, shaking off the last man to cling to him.

Lou Dikkon blocked his escape and, taking his hand, she led him back into the operating room. At sight of it, his nostrils flared, and a dull light glowed in his eyes; but at her direction he lay down again on the table, and he allowed her hands to tie on him the bonds which had driven him frantic before. Then she explained the process of anesthetizing as well as she could.

It was plain that all was a cloud to his weak understanding. But he clung to her hand and fixed his great doglike eyes upon her.

"It's all right, Lou?" he asked her.

"It's all right," said she.

She stood by with her hand resting upon his shoulder, and so stood while he lay without the slightest motion of resistance. She grew dizzy with the fumes of the ether; the doctor pronounced the state of unconsciousness complete, and she was allowed to leave the room. But as she reached the door, a shout and a sudden struggle called her back.

The giant had ripped across the cloths which tied his hands, and four men vainly were striving to keep him from sitting up.

Lou hurried back, and in a few seconds the patient lay passive under her hand.

"It seems," said the doctor in deep bewilderment, "to be rather hypnosis than ether. You'll have to stay here, my dear young lady!"

Stay there she did, and closed her eyes to keep out the sight of what was being done. But she could not keep out the sound of hammer on chisel head, or the hideous dull noise of chisel on bone, or the sound of the saw, or the low voice of Doctor Mansfeld pointing out details to his assistant as he proceeded.

Once, indeed, she opened her eyes. There was a whirl of confusion, in the midst of which the doctor raged with terrible fluency and volume. Black mists rose before her eyes. But then she steadied herself and clutched her fingers deeper into the quivering muscles of Barney's shoulder.

After that, there was quiet again. She began to reel with weakness.

"Lou!" said a choked voice.

"Steady, steady!" she murmured.

The giant was still once more, and her heart leaped with a wildly selfish joy. He had spoken her name—her memory, then, had not been wiped out!

But still the work went on, and the long silence continued. Still she dared not look. And perhaps this doctor with his demoniac skill was taking her out of the soul of poor Barney Quince with chisel and saw!

She felt there was something of devilish magic in this labor of Mansfeld's. But in the meantime, she was chained to her post, though her knees began to tremble.

Then a hand touched her shoulder, and a voice said quietly, "Drink this, Miss Dikkon!"

She looked up into the face of the doctor. His bristling, wax-tipped mustache, his glittering eyes, and his pointed beard made her feel that she was staring at some devil incarnate. She drank what he held at her lips—something pungent and stinging.

"Courage!" he said. "Without you, we can do nothing! Courage and strength, my dear child!"

He patted her shoulder, but she knew that there was no kindness in the touch. It was totally perfunctory. She happened to be, to him, a necessary instrument at this moment. And therefore she was worth conciliation—until the work had ended. But the drink gave her fresh strength.

Another long dreary interval passed.

A buzzing came in her ears, and through the buzzing a voice boomed, distantly: "She's going to faint, I think."

"Let her faint—the job's finished!"

That was the voice of Mansfeld, like the booming of cannon. Afterwards, faint she did, and felt arms receive her; but she shook off the weakness instantly as she heard a groan from the man on the table. That was the shock that cleared her brain again and enabled her to stand to her task.

Someone was explaining something to her.

Ah, yes! The operation was finished. It was successful! Now if she would walk beside the stretcher as they carried the patient only into the very next room—

She walked beside it with fumbling steps; fresh, untainted air blew about her from the open windows; and then she was sitting beside the bed of the patient.

Up and down the room walked Doctor Mansfeld.

He was speaking. She heard only snatches, as he talked about difficulties—uncertainties—pressure on the brain—the brain itself—the mystery of thought—

She hardly knew what all these long combinations of words meant; but she knew that she was ordered to sit quietly there.

She was willing to do that, for the face of the sleeper wore, in flashes, the same beautiful smile with which she was so familiar; and, when he awakened, surely he would be the same!

He stirred.

"He's going to waken," snapped the incisive voice of the doctor. "Now, my girl—you're fond of this fellow. Then lean over him. Imagine you're facing a camera. Look pleasant, please, and—"

The eyes of Barney Quince opened. They were no longer blank but filled with a wildly delirious light.

"Steady, Jerry—steady, you old fool—" And then the voice rose to a great shout.

Barney Quince sat up in bed.

"Hello, hello!" he murmured. "That was a crash and—who are you?" he asked, and looked straight into the face of Lou Dikkon.

• 6 •

SOMEHOW SHE WAS OUT OF THE ROOM AND FEELING HER way blindly down the stairs. At the bottom, brilliant sunshine blazed before her. She put her hand to her face and found it wet.

"I mustn't cry," she said aloud, and feebly, "I've got to be steady, steady!"

So she took a firm hold on herself, and made her step light as she reached the street. A shadow came up beside her and took her arm.

"What happened?" asked her father.

She clung to him weakly.

"Get me home—I'll try to talk there," she said.

So they hurried together, but it seemed that the little village street had been stretched out to weary, stumbling miles before the familiar door of the house opened to them.

She lay on the parlor couch, her eyes closed, and her father holding her hand.

He was saying very gently: "It was too bad. I didn't want the chance to be taken. But he said it was only one in ten, you know. And, after all—poor fellow! What was there in life for him, Lou? I'm sorry too, though. It chokes me, actually. There, there, honey! You cry. It'll do you good."

She shook her head.

"It isn't what you think," she managed to say. "He's alive, but he's worse than dead to all of us. He's forgotten me. He's the old Barney Quince!"

In the hospital, the doctor ordered quiet, and when he heard that sharp, incisive voice of the patient, he leaned above him and said in a tone of command, "Quince, you're all right, now. You've had a bad accident. You'll have to lie still now. In two weeks, perhaps, you'll be able to leave. Perhaps a month. Perhaps ten days. You seem to have the strength. But now, you'll have to lie still. Do you understand?"

Barney Quince looked at him from thoughtful eyes and said nothing at all.

But he obeyed the orders with the strictest patience and for many and many a day he lay still and studied the ceiling and spoke not at all, except to say good morning and good evening.

Then the doctor came back. He had been away on a brief excursion, and he visited his patient before the next mountain trip was undertaken.

He came in cheerfully, and found himself looking down into a pair of stern and quiet eyes. It seemed to the doctor that never before had he looked at a face so heroically formed for strength, or so beautiful in feature.

"Well, Quince," said he, "how are you?"

"Able to ride, thank you," said Barney Quince.

"As soon as this?"

"I'm able to ride," repeated the patient.

"Perhaps in a short time, but not yet. Has the time gone slowly with you?"

"No," replied the other, "because I've lain here and had a chance to think things out—only there's a lot that I can't piece together.

"Have you asked any questions?"

"No."

"None?" exclaimed the doctor in astonishment.

"People always tell you what's really worth hearing and

good for you. And the other sort—why, it ain't worth asking
for, is it?''

The doctor smiled a little at this rather profound philoso-
phy.

Then he sat down and lighted a cigar.

"What do you last remember—before you came to," he
asked of the patient.

"I remember my horse sliding down a bank and losing his
balance when the pebbles began to slip under him. Then I
crashed. It was like being hit hard on the point of the chin.
That was all. After that, I woke up here.''

The doctor nodded.

"Nothing in between?"

"No."

"Not a thing, then?"

"No, it's a blank."

"Shall I fill in the blank for you?"

"If you want to."

The doctor began to drum the tips of his fingers against
the arm of his chair, always regarding his sick man with an
intent gaze.

"You'd better find it out for yourself," said he. "It may
be a lot better that way. Do you know where you are now?''

"I got an idea."

"What is it?"

"It's a thing that I don't like to talk about."

"Ah?"

"Because I figure that I'm in Adare."

"It's true."

"And I'd rather be in any other place."

The doctor nodded.

"I've heard a little bit about the trouble between you and
these townsmen," he admitted. "But now I want to give you
a little advice that isn't exactly medical. You can't leave this
place, Quince. They've put guards under your window and
at your door. You have no weapons. And the thing for you
to do is to stand your trial like a law-abiding citizen. Face

justice, Quince. It's always the best way. Forget your old life, and prepare yourself for a new one.''

Barney Quince smiled, but his only answer was to ask, quietly: ''Where would I be tried?''

''Here in Adare, of course.''

''The judge would be a Dikkon,'' said he, ''and all the jury would be their men.''

Doctor Mansfeld rubbed his chin and found no more to say; he received the thanks of Barney Quince, and presently he squared his shoulders in the outer day and turned his thoughts to the upper mountains. He had done his work and he had done it well; as for the consequences, after all, he could not pretend to be both a doctor and the body of the law!

So Barney Quince was left alone, and now that he knew the situation he was in, he adapted himself to it as swiftly as he could. The doctor had ordered another fortnight of absolute rest for his patient, and the men of Adare were not prepared to arrest their enemy until the medical man had pronounced him fit to go to jail. This much they would make sure of, lest afterward the law should be brought down upon their own heads. In the meantime, they kept their guard in place, changing it at regular intervals.

It was a costly business to tie up so much man power, but the expense of it and the trouble were small things to them. The important point was that Quince lay in their power, and therefore they made the net strong and waited with unwavering patience for the appointed day.

In the meantime, Barney Quince was laboring to bring back the strength which he had lost by lying so long prone. It was no easy task, for a dozen times by day and a dozen times by night the door of his room would be softly opened and some one would look in upon him silently, and silently the head would be withdrawn after making sure that all was well. He could not even be sure of the intervals between these observations. Sometimes he might have two hours free from disturbance. Sometimes not two minutes elapsed between the spying glances that were turned upon him.

To encounter this crafty observance, he used the utmost patience. Lying in his bed, he went regularly through small movements which would exercise his muscles—such as arching his body on head and heels, or thrusting himself up from his spread arms, or lifting both legs and keeping them raised until the great thigh muscles shuddered with effort.

All of these things he could do with movements which were utterly noiseless and which needed hardly the slightest disturbance of the covers of his bed, and the result of these patient exercises was that his strength gradually returned to him, his chest arched, and power tingled down his arms to the tips of his fingers.

Yet, with that strength regained, it was no easy matter to use it for his escape. He lay on his side at the edge of his bed and scanned the ceiling and the wall. They were of smooth, newly made plaster and could not be broken without noise.

Then he stole to the window at midnight and looked down to the street. It was a sheer descent of twenty feet, much too far to be jumped; and just opposite he saw two riflemen seated, waiting patiently, should he attempt to climb down, both wide awake even at this hour.

So the window and the ceiling and the walls were hopeless as outlets, and beyond the door waited the second guard.

There remained the floor. It was of tough strips of pine, held down with new nails and covered, in part, with a rag rug.

Through that floor, nevertheless, he knew that he must go, and constantly it was in his thoughts. He had one tool: a pocketknife which they had disdained to deprive him of, because the longest blade was well under two inches in length. However, with that tool he had finally determined to attack his problem.

To be sure, the blades were short, but they were wide and strong, and made of the very finest steel, with chisel edges. So he fell to work.

Lying on his side, the cot was so very low that he could

reach the floor with either hand. He turned back the rag rug and began his work.

If three of the sections of the boards could be cut through and lifted out, there then would remain beneath him the lath and plaster work of the ceiling below. But the laths would cut through quickly enough, he could be sure.

So he started his work, conscious that there were two great dangers to its consummation—one was the fear that the spies at the door might look in upon him and find him at his labor. The second was the terror lest the rag rug should be stripped off the floor and taken out to be beaten.

On Saturdays that work was usually done. This was Tuesday on which he commenced his work, and he must trust that the daily sweeping would be done without disturbing the rug too much.

As for the constant spyings, he trained himself to baffle the spies. He never worked except during daylight, and then with one eye he constantly regarded the knob of the door. It was kept so well oiled that it could be turned without the slightest sound, but it could not be turned without the motion becoming visible. So, watching that, the instant there was the slightest disturbance the rag rug was jerked back into place, and the prisoner-patient was discovered lying on his face on his cot.

This required that his nerves should be drawn to the breaking point at all hours of the day, but it was a price which he had to pay and he paid it willingly.

As for the cuts which he made in the boards, the long strips of the tough wood that he whittled away were tucked into the mattress on which he lay, for he had made an opening in a seam for that very purpose. He made the cuts very wide, which facilitated rapid cutting; but the instant the rug was moved he would be discovered. It was a peril which he had to accept.

He did the cutting, first, at the point which he had chosen farthest down from the head of the bed. It required until Wednesday night to complete that work. Then he attacked the upper cut and went through it in a single day of hardly interrupted labor. And still he had all Friday before him—his escape he planned for Friday night.

Then, as he tucked the last shaving into the mattress, and with a smile patted down the hard little lump of wood which had been formed there under the seam, the door opened with its usual softness. Eustace Dikkon entered and came to the bedside, and with him was a spectacled gentleman. The latter set out stethoscope, thermometer, and the rubber tubing of the instrument for taking blood pressure. Then he began his examination and went over every inch of the leonine body of the sick man.

Eustace Dikkon, in the meantime, stood by with no expression in his rocklike face.

"Temperature normal," said the doctor. "Pulse normal and strong. Heart excellent. Blood pressure normal. Muscular condition excellent, in fact, I've never heard of a man in bed so long whose muscles retained their temper so well! I should say, Mr. Dikkon, that this man is perfectly sound in every way—infinitely above the average. He's in a supernormal state of health!"

Eustace Dikkon let his eyes rest for a single instant on the face of the captive, and never was malice and determined hatred more plainly visible. That single, glowing glance, and then he withdrew from the room.

In the meantime, young Barney Quince lay rigid in the bed.

Somewhere out of the distance a clock was striking. He never had heard it before, but now all his faculties were roused by excitement to a supersensibility, and he told off the faint pulse of the sound.

It was ten o'clock, and as fast as Eustace Dikkon could prepare adequate quarters in the jail, he, Barney Quince, would be brought there to wait for his death!

•7•

A STIR BEGAN IN THE HOTEL—A PASSING OF MANY FEET to and fro, and the sound of subdued voices in the halls; and the sharp creaking of the stairs under the weight of people who hastened up and down.

Barney Quince slipped softly from his bed and from the closet took shirt and trousers and stepped into them. As for shoes, he was better without them, for his purposes. And then, as he turned from the closet, the door of the hall yawned open swiftly and silently, and a great shaft of light beat into the room. His first impulse was to leap straight at the spy; but softly the door was shut again; and he heard no sound of hurrying feet, or any exclamation.

Might it not be that, glancing at the ruffled clothes of the bed, the watcher had told himself that Barney Quince still was there? A thousand times they had looked in, in this fashion, and a thousand times all had been well. However, there must be no such sudden interruption as this in the moments that followed.

He picked up the one chair, stealing close to the wall— where there is far less chance that a floor would creak underfoot—went to the door and, with the greatest care, braced the back of the chair under the door knob. He then returned to the side of the bed and threw back the rag rug.

There was a dim light faintly filling the room, from the great gasoline lamp which burned until midnight over the entrance to Whitney's stables, across the street. By that light, as he raised the pine board through which he had cut, he could examine the work which remained under his hand. The lathing was wide but the strips were thin, as if made to order for his purpose.

All the great power of his wrist went into his work as, making the notches wide, he labored around the edge of the gap in the floor. There were a hundred grittings of the knife against the grains of the plaster; twice the blade squeaked in the wood; but the disturbances continued throughout the hotel and the noises he made were, apparently, confused with what was heard elsewhere.

Once or twice he paused to listen, and in those pauses he was aware of subdued murmurs in the hall outside his room, murmurs of many men gathering there; so it was certain that Eustace Dikkon was making surety doubly sure by marshaling a little army to conduct the prisoner to the jail.

Then a sharp crunch of wood against wood. The door had been thrust in, but the chair stuck at once, and yielded, screeching, only a bit.

"What the devil is this?" exclaimed a roaring voice. "What deviltry is up here? Some of you boys put your shoulders against that door!"

Barney Quince was in a whirl of rapid action.

The upper layer of the laths he had cut through. What remained below, beside the tough plaster, he could not guess. He swept the spread from his cot and wrapped it around his bare feet; then he leaped into the air to the full of his power and brought down his two hundred pounds and the full drive of his stamping legs in the center of the hole.

There was a crash in answer, and a great sagging beneath him; at the same moment the door was struck by the weight of several strong men, yielded, then jerked open, the chair skidding before it, and half a dozen of the possemen spilled headlong into the room.

Again Barney Quince leaped, and this time he drove straight through the lathing and the plaster work beneath him; down he dropped as through a trapdoor. The rough edges of the lathing rasped at his clothes, ripped his body; but he fell headlong on the floor of the room beneath.

It was an unoccupied bedroom, as he saw when he sprang to his feet and shook the dust from his face. Above him, pandemonium was breaking loose; feet were thundering on the stairs, voices shouting.

He leaped to the door; it was locked fast!

Then, glancing upwards, he saw an arm ending in a revolver reach down.

It was like the flash of a spur in the eye of a frightened horse. Sideways Quince sprang at the door, and it split before him as though it were thinnest cardboard. Into the hallway he stumbled, and lurched straight into the arms of two men who had turned onto the landing of the stairs at full speed.

They clung to him valiantly, but his impetus carried all three over the brink of the stairs and brought them whirling and crashing down.

In a way, it was as though Barney Quince were the core of a rolling ball. The impacts which he might have received were muffled by the bodies of those who clung to him, and as that spinning mass of humanity crashed against a lower, angling wall and lay still, Barney Quince rose from it to his feet, and the other two lay motionless.

Something glimmered on the landing. He scooped it up, and now he stood armed with a loaded Colt; and half the barrier between him and freedom already crossed!

He was in a place of utmost peril, however. From the stairs above him a flood of armed men were descending, swerving around the landing places, thundering on the steps; and just below him the narrow lobby of the hotel was alive with men who had rushed in from the street. There was no escape by turning and striving to shoot his way through the numbers above him, but in the confusion beneath there was some hope.

The central light which hung from the lobby ceiling was quivering back and forth in a slow arc, so greatly had the old building been shaken by this turmoil. One shot from his Colt shattered it to bits and a shower of burning oil flamed wildly down over the heads of those beneath.

Yells of terror and pain went shrieking up; to either side the men of the clan split back; and through the narrow channel between them, Barney Quince fled on racing, naked feet.

Straight in his face, and from either side, half a dozen guns belched fire at him, but those shots were aimed by guess and from quivering hands, and the target was running like a stricken deer.

He leaped through the doorway, swerved, but the speed of his going made him lurch over the side of the front veranda. He landed in the soft, pulpy dust, and so darted around the corner of the hotel.

Before him rose a tall board fence, a wall of blackness. A bullet jerked past his ear with a rising whine. With a bound and a throwing of his body to the side, Barney Quince rolled over the top of that fence and dropped into one instant's freedom from peril in the dark beyond.

· 8 ·

No, HARDLY A SINGLE INSTANT OF SAFETY WAS WITH HIM.
Around the front of the hotel the pursuit was spilling, and
though these clansmen had been unsteadied hitherto by the
surprises with which they had been confronted, he knew that
thereafter their aim would be almost as deadly as by day.
Also, he heard the back door of the hotel crash wide, and
the heavy impact of many of the pursuing men who leaped
clear of the rear stoop and landed on the ground beyond.

A brief instant of confusion covered the eyes of Barney
Quince as with a veil; then his head cleared and he ran on-
wards.

He could run fast and far, but just beyond the village lay
rough ground that would cut his feet to ribbons; and besides,
what is the speed of a man on foot compared with the speed
of a running horse? And horsemen would begin to rush out
from the town of Adare to find him. They were mounting
now in the street; the thunder of hoofbeats were beginning,
and the yelling of the riders!

He went straight on, crossing the vegetable garden, in
which his feet drove ankle-deep through the soft sod; then,
swinging in a high vault over the fence beyond, he found

himself in a little corral; half a dozen horses leaped and rushed to the farther side of the enclosure.

And out of the distance behind him: "He's at the horses!" yelled a voice. "Chuck! Toby! Come on, boys! Don't give him time to saddle!"

Time to saddle?

No, there was not a second to be spared for that, but crouching in the shadow of the fence, like a panther in a cattle-yard, Barney Quince eyed that frightened knot of horseflesh. He saw one arched crest that lifted above the others and he knew that whether he lived or died it must be upon the back of that horse.

There was no time for a hesitating, gentle approach, no time for a soothing word; he had to accost that group of horses like a charging beast. If he reached his target with his spring, then a ghost of hope could rise in him once more. If he missed, he was a dead man, and he knew it well.

So he leaped from the fence shadow and darted forward. They split before him, rearing and squealing in their haste, but past a snaky head that snapped savagely at him he swerved and saw his chosen horse plunging to get through the mass and escape.

He aimed for the mane with his hands and missed it, but as he leaped, his legs coiled around the shuddering loins of the horse, and a squeal of terror answered him.

He was nearly torn from his place by the lunge of that great animal; and a smaller gelding went down before the giant.

But Barney Quince was in the seat, now, and one hand was twisted deep in the flying mane as the big mare hurled himself into the air.

"He's got a horse! By heaven, he's got Christie!" shouted some one from the fence top, and a gun flashed and a bullet sang.

Aye, they shot close to the mark by day or by night, the clan of Dikkon, but the great glimmering bay whirled Barney Quince around the corral like a flying comet.

She crashed through the scattering herd again and he was

nearly torn from his place as she plunged clear, bucking madly still. No stirrup or girth or pommel to cling to, no spurs to lock in the cinches, no cantle to keep him in place, still he clung like a bit of her own flesh, and she flashed around the circle again.

It was a maelstrom of wheeling, squealing horses; a thick cloud of dust darkened the air like a fog; but guns flashed through the mist; and there was the groan and fall of a stricken horse.

What purpose, however, in milling here, while the clan gathered around the corral? And yet how to break free? Certainly no kind hand would set the gate ajar for him!

He transferred his gun to the hand which was tangled in the mane. Then he reached back with his free fingers and sank them back like teeth of iron in the soft flesh of his mount's flank. He closed his hand, and turned it. The result was a veritable scream of agony from the tortured mare and she flung straight away at the fence.

It was built high to hold wild creatures from the plains, and none wilder than she ever stood within it; yet she soared at it like a bird. Her heels cracked in a sharp tattoo on the upper bar, and then she was over and rushing faster than the wind across the open ground beyond.

Bucking could not dislodge this torturing devil that clung to her; then she would daze and bewilder him with the sheer speed of her flight.

Yes, like an arrow she drove through the darkness.

A black cloud rolled before them—trees, and no reins to turn the flying mare!

So, clinging close, Quince leaned far over and prayed for luck. Boughs reached him like tearing hands; branches scourged his face like the lashes of whips, but they were through.

Before them water flashed, but the mare rose nobly at it. A broad, pale face, it gleamed below them—she was across, with the shock on the farther bank that nearly tore Barney Quince from his place. Then, scrambling catlike up the slope, she broke through the farther screen of trees—and before them rolled the hills, and the sacred heads of the mountains high against the stars!

Still she flew, and Quince laughed with savage joy as he felt her speed. Let them try to follow, no matter how light their weights, how good their saddles, how keen their horsemanship! For where is there a saddle so good as fear! Where is there a spur so sharp as utter terror?

Then he began to soothe her with a gentle voice, his hand on her neck, and then passing gently back over the flank which he had torn at with his grip of iron. She heeded nothing; she was sleek, dripping, slippery with sweat; foam flew whitely back from her mouth, open as though a cruel curb were tearing at it.

So they rocked over the hilltops, and pitched wildly down into the hollows. Not till the first long slope of the upper mountains rose before her did the mare's gallop slacken, and fall first to a staggering canter, then to a trot.

She was beaten at last, but only after such a burst as those hard-riding men of Adare never could match with their best and bravest!

From a wall of the gulch up which they were passing, Quince tore a long arm of trailing vine; of this he made a rope which he knotted about the mare's neck, and then slipped to the ground.

She came to a dead halt, head down, ears falling loosely forward, legs braced.

He felt her heart; it thundered with a rapid hammering against his hand, jarring his whole arm and body. A little more and she was dead!

He had to beat her down to the edge of the boiling creek; once there, she stood shuddering, sagging at the knees, untempted by the cold water that foamed under her very muzzle.

He began to wash her down, whistling a little, to occupy her attention while he swished the cold water over her legs, over her neck, and then gradually rubbed down her body. For a long and aching time he labored over her, until at last she gathered her legs under her and reached for the water.

He allowed her only a swallow; then dragged her tired head away and walked her up the canyon floor.

Every few minutes he paused and rubbed her vigorously again; then he passed on, tugging her after him. There was not strength enough in the vine-rope. He had to drag her by the mane, and sting her flank with his open hand to keep her in motion.

It seemed that she never would come back to herself!

Then the gray of the dawn began as they climbed wearily out of the canyon head and reached an upper table-land which made one mighty shoulder of old Mount Chisholm.

There he paused, regarding the mare anxiously as the light grew. She was a red bay, long-necked, deep of barrel, with herculean quarters fit to bear the burden of the world, as it seemed; and she seemed to have forgotten already, in her great and generous heart, the terror which she had felt for him.

When he stood close, she laid her head against his breast and sighed like a weary child.

It seemed to Barney Quince, as he stroked her wet neck, that all the adventure of his stay in Adare—that strange and cloudy stretch of months of which he had no memory—and the fall in the mountains, and the labor of his escape with all its perils had been preordained merely to bring into his hands this peerless creature.

He tore up some bunch grass and offered it to her.

Twice she sniffed it, and turned her head away.

He ripped up a bit more choice, dew-moistened. And this time she nibbled at it with feeble interest and her ears raised and stiffened a little.

Barney Quince stood back from her and laughed aloud. For he knew that that long battle for her life was ended, fought and won!

From the next runlet he let her drink, but not her fill. Instead, he pulled her head away and went on slowly.

In the back of his brain there was a great weariness, but he kept it out of his consciousness; and all that he could be aware of was freedom, sweeter than wine to his taste!

He kept steadily on, but when he came to a tempting bit of pasture, he paused a little and let the mare graze, which she began to do greedily. She was coming back to normal rapidly. Her back no longer was partly arched, her belly no longer tucked up and gaunt, and though she stumbled now and then, when he had rubbed her down with twists of grass as the sun rose, nearly her whole strength seemed to have come back to her.

He turned, then, high on the shoulder of Chisholm, and looked far down into the valley of Adare; he could not see the town, because it was blanketed with blue morning mist, but the church steeple rose like a narrow blade of light.

Barney Quince looked full in the flaring face of the sun, and he laughed again.

·9·

THERE WERE FIVE SHOTS REMAINING IN THE REVOLVER OF Barney Quince. With those five shots he killed a partridge and a rabbit the first day. The second day two more rabbits had to go to fill his hungry maw. On the third day he ate nothing at all but stalked ceaselessly to find bigger game. On the fourth day he slipped like a snake through a thicket and put a bullet into the heart of a deer just as it gathered its legs to leap.

For a week he lived on that meat and nothing else, and in the meantime he lavished his time on Christie.

It had taken her several days entirely to recover from the terrible strain of that flight from Adare, but now her full strength was back; she had forgotten the agony of fear with which that ride began; she remembered instead the care and the kindness and the deep, soothing voice of the man in the time of her exhaustion. For let no one think that a horse cannot respond soul to soul, the animal to the man, both linked together by one common element of the divine. Christie had found her master, and she knew it with a profound certainty.

It was easy to teach her. She would follow Quince uncalled by the end of the second day; by the end of a week she would

stand where he left her, grazing only in a small circle. At the
pressure of his hand on the nape of her neck and the sound
of a certain whisper, she would lower her sixteen-three of
might and muscle to the earth and lie still, head stretched
forth upon the ground.

In the meantime, he trained her for mountain work. Indeed, mountain-bred and mountain-made, it was not difficult
for her to walk on a narrow ledge, or slide down difficult
slants, or pick her way among the sharp-toothed rocks. But
though she improved greatly under his tutelage, still he knew
that with that length of limb, that mighty bulk, she never
would be a true mountaineer. She lacked that deerlike activ-
ity which is essential. The quick ups and downs broke her;
her wind left her in the labor of handling her own weight.

No, she was meant not for dodging in and out along the
coast, fighting the tidal roughs, clipping up narrow rivers and
bays, skimming through shallows, turning in her own length,
tacking like a restless midge; instead, she was meant for the
open, like a great square-rigged clipper cleaving a way from
China to the Thames. And when once her swinging stride
was driving her without effort, regardless of two hundred
pounds in the saddle, running at half her power, she could
leave gasping and heartbroken behind her the very same catlike mustangs which would catch her in no time among the
hills.

These things Barney Quince pondered darkly.

Those mountains were to him as home and the home
grounds to most men. They were to him walls of safety, and
the narrow and twisting ravines, and every cave, and every
pothole, and the condition of every run in dry weather and
wet, and all states of the passes according to the seasons, and
all the upper trails, iced or piled with snow, were printed
legibly in his memory. As it were, he turned the pages of a
book, and read at will.

Should he abandon this, it was much indeed that he gave
up.

He knew the valleys also, and the wide deserts and the
rough, inhospitable plains into which they merged, chopped

with sharp-edged draws, broken now and again by the high, ragged head of a mesa. But traveling there was different. He knew the water holes and he knew many of the people, but the region was not so thickly dotted with his friends as were the mountains, where a few dollars spent with wise caution here and there ensured him of safe harborage and true friendship. On those perilous plains below, his enemies could hunt him glass in hand, and dull beyond imagining would be the eye that failed to recognize the looming outline of Christie with such a rider on her back!

There would be need of all her speed, down there, he had no doubt. And they would bring out their thoroughbreds, their flashiest speedsters to catch him; they would send afar off to experienced manhunters and mount them with the best and send them out to run him in relays.

Well, lying on the edge of the table-land that juts out like the prow of a ship on the ridge between Lorimer Mountain and the Little Standup, he studied the lowlands for a hundred miles beneath him; and then he sat up and set his teeth.

He was going down, and let the Dikkon clan beware of his coming!

He started straight back for Adare, reached a thicket a few miles from it an hour before sunrise, and camped there for the day. Then he went on again when the night had gathered.

It was the first time that he had come to pillage in the town itself; he had struck here and there on the outskirts. He had plundered outlying ranch houses of size. But he had not made his mark in the center of the town itself. The danger had seemed too great!

However, on this night he walked on into the village, with Christie left in a clump of poplars on the verge of the place.

Now he looked about him with a calm eye of possession. To his distorted reason, all that he saw was as good as his. For, surely, it was true that the clan of the Quinces once had been stronger in numbers, richer in horses and land, than ever were the Dikkons; but in the bitter warfare back in Kentucky, by craft, by cunning guile, by the subtlety and the silence of Indians, by gathering in numbers and striking at

few, the Dikkon clan had beaten down his own, harried them
out of the country, sent them almost beggars into the West.

Then, with deathless malevolence, they had followed, and
once more the Quinces were ruined. It was something like
the story of Hydra—and when one head of a Dikkon was cut
off, two new ones came to take its place. Where he had killed
some famous fighting man of the Dikkon name, two stalwart
sons now were growing to maturity, seasoning their hatred
for him, and practicing with their guns. For nearly fifteen
years, now, no target had seemed worth while to any Dikkon
save the target of the living Barney Quince.

And all his wounds of knife and bullet burned in him, and
printed their pattern anew with an electric tingle.

He went straight down the middle of the central street.
There were lights in the hotel and saddled horses standing in
front of it—no doubt a late game of poker was dragging on
there.

And the long rays gleamed upon him as he went past; and
he felt the lightness of his empty Colt; but still he did not
dodge into the shadows; skulkers are the first seen and the
first shot at!

He came before the big store, calmly turned the corner of
the building, and at a side window he tried his handpower.
The window was latched, but the latch was weak and rusted;
it gave with a sudden snap and squeak under the pressure and
slid up.

He waited, his head canted toward the ground, but he heard
no sound.

So he slipped through the window, and carefully closed it
again. It was pitch dark, of course, inside the room, so he
lighted a match, and by its first glare he scanned the near-by
counters and the loaded shelves behind him.

Clothes—but he could attend to clothes and shoes later on.
What he wanted now was guns and ammunition, and he began weaving back and forth among the corners straight to the
far end of the store. There he laid his hand upon a barrel of
cold steel.

And then he stopped and straightened, struck with a sudden wonder.

Surely he never before had been in that store. How did it chance, then, that he had found the gun racks? These were the rifles. Then where were the revolvers?

In his mind a picture seemed to rise—the revolvers were ranged on a rack just opposite, behind his back. He turned, groping in the dark, and laid his hands instantly upon them!

Sweat stood on the forehead of Barney Quince! It was, indeed, as though some ghostly voice had guided him and guided him aright!

Ammunition, then? Well, try the second counter over, to the right, and under it, in cases.

His hands were instantly upon the boxes. He loaded the two new Colts—he was so perfectly familiar with the weapons that indeed he could take them apart and assemble them in the utter dark—and then he searched for a cartridge belt—two rows of pockets in it, the lower for rifle cartridges, the upper for revolver. Somehow, he knew that he had seen them lying on a counter—yes, just behind the ammunition layout!

And there, indeed, they were! He filled the belt; he gathered up his revolvers and the comfortable length of the rifle, and went to the clothing department again.

He had more difficulty, there, and he had to risk the lighting of a dozen matches before he had found what fitted him; shoes were even a greater labor; the lapse of time began to tell upon him, and the nerve strain made his hands tremble. But he was equipped from head to foot at the end of an hour. Slicker, boots, underwear, socks, shirts, a pair of good blankets, a Stetson, some silk bandannas, and the guns.

He went back to the other counter and dropped some extra cartridges into his pockets. One never could have too many! And then he heard the noise of a key, fitted ever so quietly into the lock of the door.

The new and heavy boots made no difference to him. Silently he stole across the store and shoved up the window without a noise equal to a whisper.

"Who's there?" called a frightened voice.

Gun poised, he turned; then he heard a stumble and a faint curse in the distance. Some nerveless watchman had seen, or thought he had seen, the flare of one of the matches that Barney Quince had lighted. Now, like a fool that holds a lantern for his enemy to shoot by, he came, announcing his coming.

But Quince was already through the window and standing safely on the ground outside when there was a flare as the big gasoline lamp of the store was lighted.

He peered in, and saw the poor watchman crouched, his rifle at the ready, peering around him at the shadows and apparently frightened almost to death.

So Barney turned away with a chuckle, and started to return to Christie. But the way was to be longer than he had planned.

· 10 ·

As HE REACHED THE BACKYARD OF THE STORE, HE HEARD the double explosion of two shots fired in rapid succession from the interior of the big building; then a window slammed wide, and a voice shouted loudly into the night: "Robbery! Thieves! Help! Help!"

Barney swung himself up to the top of the board fence and hung there, regardless of the dangerously clear silhouette which he cast against the stars for any watcher, any chance prowler. He waited, listening eagerly for the result of his mischief-making to become apparent.

Presently there were answers from up and down the street, and almost at once the spatting of rapid hoofs in the dust; no doubt the gamblers at the hotel had responded to the call. Windows began to open, and doors were slammed; he heard distinctly fragments of conversation as men strode up the street, and he heard deep cursings.

The men of Adare seemed incredulous. It was not possible in their eyes that any man should dare to invade their precincts, their innermost circle, to plunder.

Very clearly he heard one prophet cry out: "If it's any one, it's Barney Quince! It's him, come back to cover his nakedness!"

Barney dropped down on the farther side of the fence and jogged comfortably on down the line of the back yards.

He was passing a vine-covered stretch of wire netting when he heard the crunch of footfalls, too soft and light to be more than half guessed at, and before he himself could swerve, a man of Adare swung around the corner. They were so close to one another that Barney had not even time to whip out a gun; instead, he darted a long left into the face of the man and then chopped a heavy right-hander on his jaw.

After that, he slipped back a little, to give the man room to fall, since fall he must—for nothing living and calling itself human, surely, could resist two blows from the fists of Barney Quince.

The other fell, decidedly, but he fell inwards, and cast his arms around Barney as though to support himself.

He was a Dikkon, Barney could have made sure by the silence and the malevolence of the fellow's fighting. He was not tall. There was only one giant in the clan. But the man was exceedingly broad, and when he fell against Barney's chest, it was though a pillar of iron had dropped against the taller man.

Then the thick, slow arms of the unknown moved around Barney Quince. He found that his left arm was bound against his side by the encircling pressure. And the other arm of the stranger was biting into his ribs. There seemed literally no end to the strength of the man. He kept throwing in fresh power until Barney felt the wind going from his great chest. And he knew with a sense of terror and of awe, that for once in his life he was overmatched in sheer, herculean strength.

His right arm was only partially imprisoned. He managed to tear it free and then, poising it, he struck. The trip hammer does not need to fall far, and neither did the leaden fist of Barney Quince. Twice and again he let it fall on the face of the squat giant, and three times he felt his knuckles bite deep and jar against bone. But the giant did not stir. He merely freshened his grip with a might that threatened to crush Barney's spinal column.

So the latter changed his aim, and drawing back that lethal

weapon, his right hand, he drove it home behind the ear of the stranger.

The latter slackened his hold; one thrust, and Barney was away from him, but still the enemy, though staggered, had not given up the battle. As a bulldog, having lost a grip, waddles steadily, resolutely in toward his foe, so this vast, squat, apelike creature came waddling toward Barney Quince.

Something like fear came into the proud heart of Barney, then; for half a dozen times he had smitten this fellow and still the man had not gone down.

He was almost tempted to draw a gun and fire, but he saw that his assailant, as though stunned, thought of nothing but hand-to-hand war, and Barney Quince disdained to refuse a meeting on any grounds to any foeman.

He fell back a little from the silent advance; then stepping in, deft and light, he brought to bear the full weight of his body and the full smash of his active arm and wrist—and felt his hand jar home on that spot known as the "button."

Solidly and with all his strength he smashed.

It was almost like hitting a rock; there was merely a small sagging of the head of this monster, while the half-broken hand of Barney Quince dropped back to his side.

It was unreal and ghastly. Quince felt his blood turn cold with the awful conviction that this could be no man, after all, but some vast and horrible gorilla which, presently, would leap on him and bury its fangs in his throat.

For still the monster did not fall, but slowly waddled toward him, extending his arms like something without sight, feeling octopuslike for his prey.

Wild terror arose in Barney Quince. He could, of course, whip out a gun and end the struggle with one well-planted shot, and against this beastlike creature he felt that gunpowder alone should be used. Yet, doubtless it was a man, and like a man it should be battled. So, his heart in his throat, he plunged swiftly in again, his teeth set and his eye narrowed.

His right arm dangled almost uselessly at his side, so terribly had the shock of the full stroke numbed it to the shoulder, but with the left he was well-nigh as strong, and with the left he smote now to the full of his great power.

Once again there was the true finding of the jawbone; and once more there was a shock as though beating against a house timber.

Quince's numbed arms swung idly, foolishly at his side; he hardly could have drawn a weapon, now, if he had tried, and certainly he could have struck no mark with any gun.

So, scorning to fly, he stood before the squat shape; and indeed, wonder and horror made it quite impossible for him to move from his place. A hundred times before, in his adventurous youth and in his manhood, he had fought with his bare hands, whether wrestling, or rough-and-tumble such as the miners delight in, or else standing off and fairly squaring away at an antagonist. And in all those years, since he was a half-grown youngster, he had not known the man, no matter how vast of bulk, who could retain his senses after being struck fairly on the jaw by his fist.

Yet here was one who had withstood two such blows as never before had he dealt—blows which, he felt, must have crushed the heads of normal men.

Half a dozen mortal seconds that squat hulk stood before him, its arms still outstretched, but its advance ended. And it seemed more terrible than all else to Barney Quince, that the figure made no outcry, no shout for help, but simply stood uncertain.

Then slowly, heavily, down upon one knee it slumped, both apelike arms fell and supported it, and Barney Quince could see that the whole bulk was wavering a little from side to side.

The second punch, then, had told the story, but with a true fighting instinct, the stranger had still presented himself as if for battle; so Barney hesitated.

If he went on, this colossus might arise and follow him. If he remained long, he would have to resume the battle; and there was nothing that Barney Quince wanted less than to taste the power of those arms a second time.

He jerked out a gun, for a tap with the long barrel of the

Colt might be decisive. But he found that the weapon hung in air; it is no easy thing to strike a helpless man.

So he turned away and ran straight toward the nearest trees—but then turned at sharp angles behind the screen of them and hurried down the line of the village houses, anxious, now, to get back to Christie, where that good mare waited for him, still without a saddle! So he cut in closer to the houses.

There was no such uproar as he had expected, after the robbery was discovered. Instead, the people of Adare appeared to be returning to their houses; only, in the distance and scattering here and there, Barney Quince made out the separate poundings of many riders, as they went on their way through the night.

He was pleased by this. In all things, the Dikkon clan worked sensibly, quietly, never making a vast uproar. Indeed, they were efficient men, efficient fighters; and, though his blood boiled at the thought that they should have destroyed another clan of such men as himself, still he knew that there was a mighty force in them. And often, it is easier for a hundred men to beat a hundred than it is for them to beat one.

At least, one mounted on such a creature as the mare, Christie!

He dipped back toward the line of the houses, therefore, bent upon gaining a saddle fit for the mare; and the first place that caught his eye was discarded for the sake of the second which was now made out against the stars in the near distance. He examined it as he came up with an odd feeling, as though he had seen it before.

And indeed, as he came closer, and saw the peculiar sway in the back of the barn, he told himself that this was long-observed before. Yes, he could swear to it; and to the right and below that sway, on this side of the roof, there was a broad patch of new, unpainted shingles.

Would that he had the daylight, now, to test the truth of what he guessed. With his hand on a corral fence, he bowed his head and let his half-wakened memory work.

Down at the left hand was the grandary—then the great barn with the work horses ranged upon the one side and the mules upon the other. There on the right was the feed shed for the winter cattle, when they were kept up, and for the milch cows. That smaller structure was the creamery where the flat tin pans stood in long, waiting rows. And yonder, above the trees, arose the pointed roof of the house itself. And beneath that roof was some delightful, some wonderful, some heart-devouring thing of beauty!

What could it be? On that point his mind was blank!

· 11 ·

LIKE SOME CREATURE WHICH CANNOT SEE BUT IS DRAWN ON by another sense, like that of scent, Quince drew nearer to the house. It was very dangerous, he knew, to linger too long close to the village of Adare, now that it had been roused against him, but he could not resist the temptation. It forced him back from the barn, and through the rear gate of the yard, and through the narrow path that pierced the vegetable garden—

And he found himself taking the close turns by instinct, as though this were a place long familiar to him.

Again and again he paused and tried to shake from him self the impulse which urged him on, and still he was forced ahead with an invincible power that led him under the edge of the outhouses which lay behind the main buildings, and across the soft lawn, and so beneath a window outside of which was a little balcony overhung with vines. He knew that that vine was starred with small pink blossoms as clearly as though the sun now shone upon it, and the sweet fragrance was familiar to him, also.

But with every breath of that perfume, the emotion drew deeper into his very soul, and he stared at the open window above him as a thief might stare at the entrance to a king's treasury.

It was not wealth of money that lay within. What it was, indeed, Barney Quince could not tell himself; but he actually laid hold upon the stout stem of the vine, as though about the venture up the stalk.

Then reason overcame the emotion.

He forced himself back from the house with a reeling brain, telling himself that he was turning mad indeed. For what could lie inside the house of any Dikkon except hatred for him, guns prepared, and bullets straightly aimed?

He made a little detour, driving himself ahead, but every step he took away from the house was a step of pain. However, still he made reason command him, and so he reached the next premises, and there he searched for a saddle and the proper equipment for Christie.

He found it with the same unerring prescience which seemed to give him sight in the dark.

He passed the barn and went to a little adjoining shed, opened the unlocked door, and found within a range of saddles. He selected one that suited his purpose, took blanket, bridle, and all necessities, and with the considerable burden, he started back toward the spot where, so long ago, he had left the mare.

It required skulking across the main street, but this he ventured over safely, with not a sound or a sight to alarm him, and came eventually close to the little poplar copse where Christie should be.

Near by, he flattened himself against the ground and listened. For the ground is a sounding board which sends out vibrations more distinctly than the thin air. Yet he heard not a sound except a faint gritting and grinding, and he took that to be the mare grazing quietly in her small preserve.

He stalked closer, on hands and knees, thrusting his new rifle before him, when suddenly the tall form of Christie appeared out of the wood, and she whinnied to him in a whisper.

Very glad was Barney Quince to spring up and throw the

saddle on her back, while she sniffed at his new clothes and tried to nip them away, to get at the man she knew beneath them. He made wild haste, for it seemed to him that he had been wandering through a region of ghosts and that the instincts which had been guiding him were such promptings as witchcraft, say, bring to light in the heart of a man.

Indeed, he was badly frightened, never so happy as when, at last, he could leap into the saddle and thrust his feet into the stirrups.

He cast one wild glance around him, and then headed Christie for the open ground.

He had half feared that the new burden might clog her speed, but he was reassured by the first stride she made. She floated away with him and all his equipment as though the whole was thistledown and she a wind to carry it!

Then the wide valley received them, and the stretching darkness lay deep and thick between them and the lights of Adare.

He drew her back now to a soft trot and still he rode with his face turned toward the village, for a strange debate was raging in him.

And reason, sternly and steadily, told him that Adare was thronged with enemies who would laugh as they killed him, as dogs pull down a wolf; and yet that blind, strange instinct with a powerful hand checked him and almost turned him back, seeming to say in the clearest of voices that behind him, in Adare, a treasure beyond counting waited for him, a treasure that was neither gold nor jewels nor horseflesh nor weapons. What it was, then, he could not imagine, but he knew that his heart leaped wildly, and a frantic joy took him by the throat.

It was as though he rode on some lofty and dizzy mountain ledge and were tempted to fling himself into the air, assured that wings would bear him up and carry him swiftly over the white summits beyond. That temptation raged like a fever in his blood, and yet common sense told him that such a flight was terrible, unavoidable death.

At last, he turned a resolute head to the front; and yet in

five minutes he had turned again and brought Christie to a halt to start at the dwindling rays of light that shone out and reached after him like hands through the darkness.

Then, desperately, he gave Christie his heel and, while she rushed at full speed ahead, he set his teeth and closed his eyes.

When he opened them again and glanced over his shoulder, all was darkness around him, and he was in the silent heart of the desert, with the feeling that he had escaped from Fate.

He had carried off a full accounterment at the expense of aching ribs where those terrible arms of the stranger in the dark had crushed him; and rarely had there been a more profitable and easy adventure.

Yet Quince was not at rest, for he told himself that Fate, after all, cannot be avoided; and if he dared to question his heart, it told him that surely, before many days had passed, he would be led back blindly to Adare—and to what awaiting him?

By the stars and by the dim front of Mount Chisholm behind him, he laid his course with surety, now, and came at the end of two hours of easy travel to a small house between the glimmering face of a great "tank" on one side and the shadowy bulk of a string of cottonwoods on the other.

Behind the house was a ragged line of sheds, and a tangle of corrals, but all was on a small scale, so that even in the night the home seemed a pitiable thing, scarcely able to endure the withering heat of the sun and the sweep of the winter winds.

He went to the front door and kicked heavily against it three times. Then he reined back and waited.

Almost at once, a voice called from an upper window.

"Who's with you, Hilary?" asked Barney Quince.

"Hey, Barney!" shouted the man of the house. "I thought we'd never have the luck to see you again. It's all safe here. Nobody but me and the girl. Feed your horse in the shed. I'll be down—"

And then as he turned from the window his voice was

heard more dimly, calling: "Marjorie! Marjorie! Hey, wake up! It's Barney come back to us!"

It soothed the puzzled heart of Barney Quince to hear this cheerful welcome. He fed Christie in the barn, and then he came back to find Hilary Clarkson hurrying toward him in the starlight.

His hand was wrung. He was led by the arm into the house, and there was pretty Marjorie, her eyes dancing, her nose a little more freckled than ever, dressed in a blue gingham wrapper. She gave him both her hands—which is not the Western way!—and then she made a tremendous racket at the stove, and half filled the air with dust as she shook the ashes from the grate. Immediately the fire was blazing, the coffee-pot was on, the frying pan began to smoke—with lightning hands a place was laid on the clean oilcloth which covered the table.

"She's great, ain't she?" said Barney Quince in admiration to the father. "What a woman she's turning out, Hilary!"

"Tell it to her," grinned the father. "She'll listen to you—maybe. Now lemme hear about yourself—and what happened to you, Barney, in Adare?"

But a shadow fell over the mind of the guest at that word. He set his jaw and frowned. Then he shook his head and made answer: "I'll talk about anything else. I don't want to talk about that!"

"Hey?" cried Clarkson. "But smashing your way right through the whole mob of them—and getting clean off, bare-back, on Steve Dikkon's best horse! The finest mare, they say, that ever stepped inside of Adare! Man, you mean that you won't talk about that?"

"I'll talk about that," said Barney slowly, "but nothing else about Adare—it makes me a little sick, Hilary. I ain't myself. My nerves are turning upside down—and I dunno what's wrong with me!"

The rancher nodded sympathetically.

"You take the life that you've been leading, and everything that's happened to you lately"—here he touched the back of his head and nodded significantly—"and it's sure to upset you some way. I tell you what, Barney, there's only one thing for you to do!"

"Well, lemme hear?"

"It's simple and plain as the nose on your face. Change your name. Go north. So somewhere on the range where nobody ever has seen your face. Start life over again, dead quiet—and ask a woman to be your wife, one that ain't afraid to rough it with you."

"Ah?" cried Barney Quince. "A woman? A woman?"

There was such a strange note in his voice that the girl by the stove started; and then bowed closer over her cookery, a deep crimson flooding her face.

But Barney Quince was looking far off, at his thoughts, and he saw nothing that lived within that room.

· 12 ·

Now, in the dark of the room which was assigned to him, he sat at the window and looked across the plain, wide and level as a sea. These faithful friends, he knew, would watch over him and guard him like a member of their family. He could remain here safely, say, until the next evening, when again there would be danger that the pursuit from Adare, passing out from that village in increasingly great circles, might reach as far as this; but safety from the pursuit of his enemies was not his concern. Safety from the assault of his own mad impulse was what haunted him.

For still he could breathe the fragrance of that shower of unseen bloom beneath the window of the unknown house in Adare, and still the memory of that perfume went into his mind like the rarest wine, and the house itself rose before the eye of his imagination, like something not once but a thousand times seen.

Yes, it seemed to him that he could have opened the side door—he knew well that the key was kept beneath the mat—and then he could have passed silently, even in the darkness, from hall to hall, until he came opposite the door of that same chamber whose window he had stood beneath.

He buried his face in his hands, for the mere thought of

the door, like the memory of the window, made his pulse leap wildly, and it was only by a vast effort of the will that he was enabled to force himself into his bed.

There he lay face down, his arms wrapped around his head to shut out the world of sight, the world of sound, the world of all imaginings!

He slept at last, but a wild and broken sleep in which he dreamed that he dreamed, and the dream became reality, and reality became the dream, so that he sat up in the morning, pale, faint, with a heart that fluttered weakly in his breast, as though he had been climbing mountains all night long.

Marjorie was already up and at work in the kitchen. She gave him a smile from an open heart, but he walked past her with a nod and went to the barn.

On the way, he passed Clarkson, who hailed him cheerfully.

Christie, at least, would be something actual, a sunlight reality!

No, when he saw her, though she filled his eye as a perfect mount, he could not help remembering that he had won her from the semi-fabulous town of Adare; and, therefore, she was a part of the dream, she was the ever-present link that connected him with the past! How had he come by her? Where would she bear him?

Back, of course, to the town! Back until he stood once more beneath that fascinating and dangerous casement, clad with vines and with immortal fragrance!

Barney Quince felt his brain reeling.

He harnessed the mare; the saddle was in his hand when he knew what he must do, and he hurried out to find Clarkson milking his one cow.

"Hilary," he said, "have you got a pony here?"

"You mean something to carry you?"

"Yes."

"I was in and looked at the mare you borrowed from Steve Dikkon," grinned the rancher, "and you'll never need a second while you've got her to carry you!"

"I want to change with you," declared Barney Quince.

"I'll trade her for any good mustang that can pack me through a day's march."

Hilary stared.

"I wouldn't have enough cash in a year's income," said he, "to pay you the boot you'd need!"

"I want no boot," said Quince bitterly. "I'll give you the mare. You give me the mustang. We'll be quits."

Clarkson shook his honest head.

"What I've done for you is too little, old man," he insisted. "You want to give me something; you ain't got the cash; so you offer me your horse. Well, that's like you! But I couldn't take her. You don't owe me a thing. Why, Barney, you've always overpaid me!"

Barney Quince grew wroth.

"I tell you," he exclaimed, "that all I want is to leave that mare behind me. I don't want her. I'm finished with her. She—I'd rather ride hell-fire than ride her!"

The rancher stared again, but with a vastly different expression. "If that's really the way of it—well, there's my string in the little pasture. You go and take what you want."

Barney Quince took a roan. It was a lump-headed creature, with a little, wicked eye; but he felt that that humor would suit him exactly.

So he packed that sturdy mustang, with the inward assurance that, if the little horse could not go fast, at least it could go far.

Then he returned to the house and, pausing near the door to scan the wide plain with a joyless eye, heard the rancher say: "I dunno what's wrong with him; he talks sort of crazy. It's the fall that he got, I suppose, and he'll never be the same man again!"

"Fall? No," said Marjorie, "it's a woman. I know! When they get that wild, sad look—they're crazy about some girl. Poor Barney!"

And again, as on the night before, an electric shock leaped through the body and soul of Barney Quince.

A woman!

He felt, indeed, as though, if a prophet had spoken out of

a holy text, there could not have been more truth. There was a woman at the base of all his trouble. And in the back of his brain, if he could make some vast effort, he would be able to visualize her features. It was the terrible and joyous hope of seeing her in the frame of the window above the balcony that had made his heart swell; it was the thought of her that had brought him to the door in the house of the stranger.

Fate, again! And yet, what a black curtain of uncertainty had fallen across his eyes!

So he went in and had his breakfast, and when it was finished he paused at the door, his quirt coiled in his hand, and leaned above pretty Marjorie.

"Marjorie," said he, "I heard you telling your father what's wrong with me. Are you sure of it?"

She, crimson, trembling, could not meet his eye, and her glance wavered from side to side.

"I don't know, Barney," she managed to say. "I don't know—you ought to know—best—yourself!"

"God bless me!" said Barney Quince. "Are you crying, really? And why? Look here, honey! The next time I come near a town, I'll find a present for you and bring it back."

The unbidden tears still streamed down her cheeks, but she clenched her hands and stamped.

"I don't *want* your presents!" she cried at him.

Barney shrank awkwardly out of the house. He did not understand; neither did he know, indeed, why Hilary Clarkson smiled grimly on one side of his face as he bade his celebrated guest adieu. But he was sure enough that all was not well between the family and himself.

He rode across the desert, aiming his course toward the pools which stand between Claverhouse Crossing and the Little Run. There he would water, rest his horse a day, and then start on through the real heat of the desert and its long, flat marches. He had only one direction in his mind, and that was away from the town of Adare on the straightest line.

He was putting between him leagues which, he felt confident, would blot from his mind the temptation which kept swelling there.

He could realize that Marjorie was right. He was in love, and for the first time. In love with a nameless thing, a ghost, a thought, a nothingness!

So, squaring his shoulders, he continued on the march, only turning, now and again, to scan the horizon behind him and all around.

It was in one of these moments of observance that he saw a group of small black spots against the sky. He paused and looked at them with the greatest care. They gradually grew larger. He made sure by the rate of their approach that they were horsemen; and with strange troops of riders he must take no chances. So he sent the mustang into a gallop and rocked steadily along over the loose sands.

For half an hour he kept up the pace and then looked back to make sure that the four specks had disappeared.

By no means! Instead of disappearing they had grown vastly larger and he could distinguish them now without the slightest trouble. Four riders, and undoubtedly mounted on blooded horses. Where could they come from, except from the town of Adare? Who could be in those saddles except men of the clan of Dikkon?

Quince trimmed himself in the saddle, and gathered in the slack of the reins; then he worked the roan hard in a straight line ahead. Now and again he threw a backward glance. The roan was running hard and true, but the four were gaining with alarming rapidity.

What were those stories of mustangs capable of dropping behind them, in the uncertain footing and the burning heat of the desert, all the well-bred horses of the world? Here, then, was the chance to prove it, for the roan was a good one of his type, hardened by constant work, with every advantage except grain in his feeding. And yet he could not stand against these rushing riders on horses with a stroke that seemed twice as long as the bobbing roan's!

They drew nearer and nearer until Barney Quince unlimbered his rifle and calculated the distance for a long-range shot. Anger and scorn began to rise in him. For surely some one among them must have a pair of glasses—and they must know that they were riding in the pursuit of Barney Quince. Since when, then, had four of the Dikkon clan dared to adventure on the trail of Barney Quince?

Turning to view them more steadily, he saw that one was a strangely broad fellow; in the distance, he seemed twice the size of any of his companions. And suddenly he knew by a certain premonition that this was his Hercules, his unknown warrior of the dark. A touch of cold ran through the blood of Barney Quince; though why he should have felt fear he could not say. The odds, at least, were not enough to disturb him; let them come within the range of his rifle and quickly he would reduce their fighting force!

• 13 •

THEY CAME FEARLESSLY ON; SO HE DREW THE MUSTANG back to a soft canter and, turning in the saddle, he raised the rifle to his shoulder. At once the four split and spread out fanwise, though they made no effort to fire with their own weapons, frankly admitting that at such range they were helpless. But Barney Quince was not helpless, and he fixed his grim eye on the squat and powerful form of his night foe.

That man gone, the three surely would think twice before they pressed him closer; so he stopped the mustang altogether, covered his man, and drew the bead so firmly that he felt as if a line were drawn from the muzzle, arching through the air, leading the bullet to the mark.

The other three were weaving their horses to and fro as they galloped, but the squat form of the stranger drove straight on, disdaining such maneuvers.

Barney Quince, feeling in his heart respect for such dauntless courage, pressed the trigger, and lowered his rifle to watch the fall; but the man did not fall. He rode on, and the wind curled and uncurled the brim of his wide sombrero.

Quince, stunned, blinded, was sure that the four could not be other than an empty mirage, still galloping closer; for it was not his wont to miss a human target! With an oath, he jerked the rifle once more into the hollow of his shoulder, took aim even more careful—and at a target how much nearer!—then fired a second time. But still the squat and mighty horseman drove on, disdaining to weave from side to side, disdaining to draw his rifle for an answering shot, though his three companions had their weapons out, now, and were pumping a shower of lead at the foeman. Barney was agape, half unnerved.

They were near enough, now, for Barney Quince to see them turn in their saddles and point to the side, and, following the gesture, he saw yet another rider sweeping over the sands, far swifter than the others. No, not a horseman, but a riderless horse which ran valiantly; and now the four swept to one side, waving their hats, shouting, as though they wished to cut off the advance of the strange horse.

They might as well have striven with a thunderbolt, for, arching out a little from the straight line of its coming, with the sun flashing on its polished flank, the great runner came for Barney Quince, and suddenly he understood. It was Christie, broken away from her new keeper and coming for her real master. Somewhere in the past he had heard of horses able to work out a trail—and no doubt she had seen the direction of his going.

But here, at least, was the miracle sweeping toward him, and the four riders hot behind her. He turned the mustang, therefore, and rode with red spurs, as fast as the short legs of the sweating horse would carry him; but now the whinny of Christie was coming up behind and soon her shadow shot over the sand beside him.

The four were hopelessly distanced by her, but still they gained fast on the mustang, and Christie began to circle around her faster in great loops, her ears flattened, curvetting high as though she threatened to dash the life from the mustang in one of these charges of hers.

So Barney Quince, to take a gift that had fallen from the sky, undid the throat-latch, undid the girths, and as they were dangling, he jerked the mustang to a halt, tore off saddle and bridle, and flung them on the mare.

The four behind knew well what that meant. They had their guns out, now, even the squat and formidable warrior; and they clipped the air about the ears of Barney Quince as he jerked the girths up and then flung himself into the saddle.

Now let them ride their best, for Christie was away like a happy arrow driven toward a mark of its own seeking, and in the saddle Barney Quince turned and dropped a pursuing horse with his first shot. The rider rolled headlong, then got up staggering, in a cloud of dust, and in another moment the remaining three drew rein, dropped from their saddles to the ground, and opened fire. The very first bullet cut through the crown of Barney Quince's hat, but luck favored him then. For, before him opened a draw just deep enough to swallow horse and man from sight, and, dipping into it, in five minutes he was safely out of range.

He came back to the upper level, then, and looking to the rear he could see the enemy gathered in a group as for consultation. With that, he put them from his mind. They had gone their best, and their best was very good, but not good enough for Christie!

He reached the water holes in the middle of the afternoon and gave the mare to drink; then he rode on and made dry camp that night in a belt of greasewood that ran out down a shallow draw, creeping like smoke on the face of the desert.

It was the loneliest night in all the life of Barney Quince. For in the other days—save long, long ago when his father still lived—there had been no human interest in this world for Barney. And even that father had been rather more of a name than a flesh-and-blood reality. He had been seen by flashes, coming and going, save on a few occasions when he returned, wounded and sick. The great work was all that occupied the mind of Barney's father—that great work of stinging the Dikkon clan like a gadfly, to madden them if he could, not destroy them. In turn, Barney himself inherited the labor of his kind and made the feud a greater thing than happiness. For happiness, indeed, was only on the Dikkon trail, gun in hand. The record of his glory was the number of notches which he was entitled to file into the butt of his gun.

And that was what humanity meant for him—gun-fodder! There were, to be sure, certain so-called friends who were scattered here and there through the mountains and the desert. He had bought their kindness, and Hilary Clarkson was the best of them; but even Hilary, Quince well knew, could not be trusted past a certain point. His price could soon be reached!

So there was no real tie between this wanderer and the whole human race; he looked upon himself not as a man, indeed, but as a highly perfected instrument of vengeance, and there was never a time when he would not gladly have laid down his life to take half a dozen lives of the Dikkon clan.

However, there was another responsibility before him, for he must not only strike in person, but also he must leave another behind him, to strike and to bear the name which he had borne. So, one day, he must have a wife—he looked forward to marriage as a necessary evil, a vast evil, and a trouble!

He who has no friends and wants none cannot be alone. But now it seemed to poor Barney, as he lay in the black hollow of the night, that one half of his soul was gone from him and stood again beneath the window of the house of the stranger in Adare.

If there were a woman, a Dikkon she must be, and how could he exchange so much as a kind word with one of that infernal breed? Yet there was a pain in his heart, aching like an old wound in cold weather until he sat up with a groan, and Christie came softly toward him, and snuffed loudly at his face.

He fell back again and closed his eyes to shut out the brightness of the stars, for they, too, were a part and a portion of the enigma in which he found himself. The world was strange to him, but far more strange than the world was the riddle of his own new-found soul. Fate, he was sure, now had taken him in her hand. All things served to show it. And no doubt what Fate meant was that he should fall soon at the hands of the clansmen.

For that matter, from his earliest boyhood he never had conceived any other end as possible, proper, or desirable. He merely had hoped to extend the blood-trail through many years; now he knew that that trail was drawing to a close!

All things pointed to it. Men have premonitions before the end. So had he! Odd things begin to happen as a stormy life draws toward the final port. Lights glimmer from the unseen shore.

So with him. With invisible noose he was drawn back toward Adare. Here was the mare from which he had separated himself, now by miracle, as it were, restored to him. And above all, there were those strange encounters with the unknown giant who had wrestled with him in the dark, who had pursued him, and had been immune before his bullets!

The eyes of Barney Quince closed a little before daybreak, but his sleep was short and troubled; and, when he wakened, he rose with the gloomy air of a man who knows not where nor to whom to turn.

So, like one who throws all burden upon chance, he let Christie take the lead, that day, and go whithersoever she would, and very glad was he that she had turned away from Adare. He let her journey on, and he was gladder still when he lost his bearings altogether, for it was a pleasant relief to cast himself upon the broad shoulders of his fate. Let it guide him where it would!

A dust storm struck them in the afternoon and gave horse and rider three wretched hours, but Christie kept steadily on, dogtrotting with a stride that made the miles drift by.

The wind fell, but now the sky was overcast, and the air still so filled with unsettled particles that it was like a dense fog through which the traveler could not see a half mile in any direction.

Darkness began, and the visibility became less and less, while Christie moved cheerfully on her self-appointed course. At last, at the top of an upgrade, in the middle of a pleasant wood, Quince made his halt for the night. In this darkness he could risk a fire with little chance of being seen, but no sooner had the flame began to take in the wood than he looked up and saw the clouds widely parting across the arch of the stars, and then a changing wind began to clear the lower air. With haste he put out the fire, and scattered earth carefully over the embers. Then he went to the edge of his little grove to look over the countryside, and gain his bearings if he could.

Straight before him rose the mass of Mount Chisholm, with its familiar square shoulder, and in the valley beneath was a huddle of gleaming lights.

Christie, swinging through a great circle, had brought him fairly back upon Adare!

· 14 ·

All that Barney Quince had dreaded before, now he knew to be the truth, and the destiny against which he had vainly fought now overmastered him. The very animal which had come into his hands and which loved him was now an instrument which brought him bodily back to his enemies, and she had saved him twice only to destroy him in the end! Now in a cold despair he surrendered his last hope and prepared himself to die.

He would not go down to the enemy as a ragged vagabond, at least. He stripped and bathed in the starlight in a little runlet of cold water. He shaved in the darkness, an operation to which he was long accustomed. Then he dressed, brushed his clothes with care, and rubbed up his boots. Finally, he rubbed down Christie, resaddled her, and rode to meet the destiny which had been hounding him.

On the way, he looked to his guns, and made sure that every chamber was loaded. There were fifteen shots in the rifle; there were six apiece in the revolvers; a heavy knife hung in the front of his belt, and as he drew nearer to the lights of Adare, he merely asked of Fate that he might be allowed to empty his guns, and then to die knife in hand, working what harm he could before the last of the clan of

Quince fell under the hands of their ancient enemies. Indeed, it seemed to him that it had long been preordained that the clan of Dikkon should triumph over its foes.

So, let come what might, he turned Christie along the back of the town until he was opposite the great outline of the barn which arose behind the house of mystery; in a thicket he left her, and for an instant leaned his head against her sinewy, silken-surfaced neck. Then he went straight toward the house.

Like a cat he walked, pausing now and again and staring through the darkness; but no trap seemed laid for him, and if he were walking upon his fate, at least the Dikkons seemed unaware of the good fortune that was about to come to them.

He crossed the fences and the garden once more. He passed beneath the trees which made a cool belt of shadows around the place, and again it seemed to Barney Quince that he could name them in the darkness—here an oak, there an elm, and there a holly bush beside the wall. He went to them and touched their leaves, and then shuddered as he realized that his guesses had been utterly correct.

A curtain was drawn up suddenly, and a column of light flared forth at him. Out of its path he leaped, and crouched in the darkness, with two guns ready in his hands. This, surely, was the end!

But no, the window was raised, creaking a protest; and the sound of the voices of men came clearly out to him. One was a deep, husky rumble; one was clear and pleasant of tone, so Quince approached stealthily and stood to listen by the window.

For that matter, when he cared to risk a glance, he could see their faces. He knew them both.

One was a man of middle age, with a brown, kindly, shrewd face which, Quince was sure, he had seen a thousand times before, though he could give it no name. But in some other incarnation, in some other life, by some division and rejoining of his spiritual being, in whatever mysterious manner, he had known that man, and the very sound of his voice, and the small white scar which flecked his right cheek.

He knew all this, and besides, he knew well the second partner in that conversation. Enormous of head, bull-throated, with shoulders as wide as a door, this was that night-fighter who had closed with him and so nearly crushed the life from his body; this was that same rider who had followed him over the desert with such remorseless courage and had made his shots fly wild!

All his great power was not his, now. There was a neat white bandage around his head, and his body, when his coat fell open, seemed oddly bundled. He lay back in a big easy chair; his face was pale, and his eyes were sunken in deep hollows.

Indeed, the first word that Barney Quince heard referred to the condition of this arch-enemy, for the older man was saying urgently: "You'd better go to bed, my lad! You shouldn't be sitting up like this. You'd better turn in and rest. The doctor—"

"I tried bed and couldn't stay there," said the rumbling voice. "I've got to be up and around. Besides, I'm only scratched, not really hurt!"

"A slash along your head and a furrow down your ribs— is that nothing, Jim? By heaven, you touched hands with death a couple of times today, old fellow!"

The other leaned backward in his chair, his face disturbed a little with pain as he stirred.

"He's beat me twice," he said slowly, staring before him with unseeing eyes. "I never thought I'd find the man that could do it! He's beat me twice!"

The older man was silent; and Barney Quince, his heart far lighter, listened eagerly. For, after all, his bullets had not missed. Each of them had touched the target, and each of them would have turned back any other man than this.

"Twice?" said the first speaker slowly. "*Twice*, Jim?"

The big fellow pointed to one side of his face, swollen and discolored.

"You mean where you tripped and fell into the lumber pile, Jim?"

"It was no lumber pile."

"What? That night the thief—"

"I met the thief."

"Hello! Do you mean it?"

"I met him; he was Barney Quince. I put my glass on him today and I knew it was him. And then we came closer, and I was surer. I've never seen him before except in the night, but I knew the cut of him. It was Barney Quince, and he was the thief. We fought, and he got in the first blow—he had that advantage."

He paused, his lips working a trifle and his big jaw muscles bulging.

"Afterwards, I managed to close with him and I got my arms around him—"

He added, after another of those eloquent pauses: "I've had my arms around men before, cousin, and I've worked through their strength, big and small, and had 'em turn to pulp. Well, I tried to break Quince in two, and I put more power into it than I'd ever tried to put into another thing. I had a reason to want him out of the way, for the minute I saw him loom in the dark, I knew that fate had put Barney Quince in my way, and if I got rid of him—"

He paused, and then lifted his head and looked keenly upwards.

"I understand," said the other. And he nodded in perfect sympathy.

The man continued, "I was putting out my full power on him, Cousin Oliver."

That name startled Barney Quince, for now he remembered it perfectly—once it had sounded in his ears. Oliver! Oliver Dikkon—a kind and a just man. How could he know both the name and the nature of this man?

"But it was like," continued Jim Dikkon, "it was like hugging a cask. The bones of my forearms ate into the ribs of him; they were like the ribs of a ship! But still I had trust that I'd break him down. Then he tore one hand free and beat it into my face three times, and three times it was like being hammered in the face with a maul. I laid my head on his shoulder, where he couldn't get at me, and at the same time, I felt his body began to sag.

"I thanked heaven. I told myself that I had won. I had a flash, maybe, of how fine it would be to bring in that grand man a helpless prisoner. Taken by one man, eh?"

He stopped again, to laugh bitterly.

"But he wasn't taken," continued the narrator. "He clubbed his fist. It was like a lump of iron, and he brought it in behind my ear. Well, it got him loose from me. Afterwards I tried to rush in, but he stood away and his fists were like cannon balls. They seemed to hit straight through my head. He dropped me and stunned me. That was the lumber pile I stumbled into, Cousin Oliver—Barney Quince!"

Down Oliver's face great beads of perspiration were rolling.

"It was as near a thing as that!" cried he. "As near as that, Jim!"

"Aye, it was."

"But at least, you got away from him; he didn't have a chance to use a gun on you!"

"I lay on my knee, sick and seein' nothing. He could have finished me then. With a gun—or a knife, maybe. Or he could have choked me. I was that soft!"

"It's not his way, after all," observed Oliver Dikkon. "Give the devil his due—he fights fairly."

"He does," agreed the giant. "There's no murder in him. I'll give him his due. That night he outfought me; and today he beat me again; but still I tell you that I have confidence, Cousin Oliver."

"Would you meet him again, Jim?" asked his cousin curiously.

"I'd meet him again and I will meet him again," replied Jim Dikkon. "I've got a sort of feeling about it. I'm gonna have him at my mercy, the way he's had me at his. And then—"

His face grew savage.

"And then?" asked Oliver Dikkon, leaning forward in his chair.

"Why," began Jim savagely, "why, I'd—"

His voice trailed off but, rallying fiercely, he said: "I have reason enough for wanting him dead, I guess?"

His glance again flashed upwards, and again Oliver Dikkon nodded in understanding as he answered: "So have all—reasons a little different from yours, perhaps."

"And still," murmured Jim Dikkon, "I dunno—I dunno—somehow I don't see the end of it!"

· 15 ·

IT OCCURRED TO BARNEY QUINCE, AS HE STOOD BY THE window, that had a Dikkon been in his place, at such a point of vantage, with two of the clan's enemies helplessly seated before him, their moments of life would have been short indeed. But he was not tempted to assassination; for, like his father before him, his battles were straightforward struggles in the open.

But however interesting might be the conversation between Oliver Dikkon and his companion, it was not to listen to talk that Barney Quince had adventured into this danger.

He left the window and returned beneath that vine-hung balcony which had clung like an obsession in his thoughts for days.

The window above was open, but all was black within, and yet it seemed to him that a transcendent joy poured out to him from above. He laid his hand on the stalk of the climbing vine. He tested its strength, and a shiver ran softly through the foliage above, but all held fast.

So, softly as he could manage it, he began to climb, and he drew himself up little by little until his hand could grip the lower edge of the balcony. Then, swinging once or twice like a pendulum, he lifted his leg over the railing and presently stood on the little platform, stifling the sound of his breathing.

Then, in the dark square of the window, he saw a form of glimmering white; like a ghost it stood before Barney Quince, and like a spirit it called to his soul. He heard a frightened cry—"Who is there?"

And he answered, half stunned with fear and wonder: "It's me—it's—"

"Barney! Barney!" cried the voice of a girl, and he thought there was both terror and joy in it. "Oh, Barney, you've come back—why are you here?"

She came closer; she stood in the window so that the clear starlight fell on her face and he could see her; and he knew that he had seen her before. This was the lovely mystery which had remained within the room, this was the thing for which he had been brought back.

It was the weight of awe that dropped upon his heart that made Barney fall upon his knees.

"Who are you?" said Barney Quince. "And who am I? And in the name of heaven, have I ever seen you before? And where? Because my brain's spinning like a top!"

"I'm Louise Dikkon. Of course you've seen me a hundred times—when you were living here."

"Dikkon!" breathed he, and the name stabbed him with a dreadful pain. "Dikkon!"

She leaned from the window, drawing a dressing gown around her shoulders.

"Barney, do you remember at all?"

"I begin to. It's all in the shadow. But I begin to remember—Lou!"

"What brought you here?" she asked of Barney.

"You!"

Her breath caught.

"They have ten armed men in the house, ready to start for you in the morning. They hate and they fear you, Barney, and if they found you here, I couldn't save you! Do you understand? You're standing over powder!"

"A man has to die some day," he answered her gravely.

"I can't keep on living forever, Lou. I've tried to ride away; I've had to come back. I've had to come back to you, Lou. And I won't leave. If they find me—then let it be the finish. What finer place could I get to die?"

She stepped through the window and stood by him, and he rose, towering above her. She caught his great arms and shook them in nervous desperation.

"I mean what I've said. They'd shoot you down with no mercy! There's nothing on earth that they'd rather do—they hate you—except my father and me. They all hate you, Barney. They don't know your kindness and your gentleness—"

"Kindness?" murmured Barney Quince, amazed. "Gentleness? Lord it ain't me that you've known but some other man!"

"Don't speak," said the girl. "They'll hear you. They'll hear you even if you so much as whisper, I think! Jim Dikkon will hear; he's not like other men!"

"Who is Jim Dikkon?"

"The man you wounded today. Don't you know?"

"And he's going to ride after me?"

"Yes, yes!"

"He came here to hunt me?"

"He came here to marry me, Barney."

"Aye," murmured Barney Quince, "I guessed there was a real reason why he needed killing!"

A door slammed heavily somewhere in the house; footsteps came up the hall and paused.

"Lou!"

At that, overcome with terror, she swayed into the arms of Barney, and clung to him; he drew her closer, and felt the warmth and tremor of her body.

"Lou!" called a voice from the hall.

Then, distinctly, they heard another say more quietly: "She's sound asleep. Let her be, Cousin Oliver!"

The footsteps retreated.

"Go now!" gasped Lou Dikkon. "You see? Jim Dikkon suspects something and he brought my father up to see if anything were wrong! He's like a hunting dog. His brain isn't like the brains of other people! Go now, Barney. In another minute it will be too late.''

He leaned above her and kissed her forehead, and then her lips; and when she tried to speak again, he kissed the words away; and that fragrance which he had breathed before now entered his very soul, never to leave it until his death day.

She, faint and pale, swayed in his arms.

"Lou, if they were to find me now and kill me, I'd laugh as I died. Why do you try to send me away? It ain't the years a man lives that counts. All the rest of my life, compared with this, why, I'd chuck it away and laugh as I chucked it. It ain't worth thinking of. I tell you, Lou, heaven, or the devil, or something sent me back to you, and I'm helpless! I can't leave you!''

"Barney,'' said Lou, pushing herself back a little to look up into his face. "I know that you love me!''

"Love is a fool word,'' said Barney Quince. "There ain't any word that could name what I feel for you, if you understand that!''

"Barney, I know that I never can care for any other man. Even when your brain was stunned and you were so like a poor child, I loved you, but I didn't know it until the doctor took you away, and the operation—''

Her voice failed.

"I'm beginning to understand things,'' said Barney Quince. "I'm only beginning to understand. This was where I stayed when I was out of my head!''

"Yes, yes, yes!''

"And I lived right here among the Dikkons?''

"My father wouldn't let them hurt you; and then—afterwards—I think every one grew fond of you, Barney. Only when they knew that you were getting well and had forgotten everything here—then they tried to take you.''

"I begin to see it! Your father kept me here?''

"More than eight months, Barney!''

"And if I'd met him afterwards, not knowing, I would have shot him down, not thinking! I tell you, Lou, let them do what they want with me, because they've had me in their hands once, and I owe them a life. D'you understand?''

''But for my sake, Barney! Go away for me, because I do love you, dear! Will you listen to me? We can arrange places to meet—and then something may happen so that we—''

''I stay here,'' he answered calmly, ''because I know that I've come to the end of one life, Lou. I can count the seconds of it running away from me like blood—d'you think that I'll give up my time with you to spend it anywhere else?''

She said in desperation, ''If you'll go, Barney—I'll do anything! I'll go with you; I'll stay with you; I'll live with you in the wilderness, Barney. Will you go now?''

''You go with me?'' he said, holding her head in his great hand. ''How would you live as I live, Lou?''

''I'd find a way. You and I together would find a way. I'm not the least afraid of that. I only know that if you stay here, they'll surely kill you; and I'll never live after you're dead, Barney. I'll never live a day!''

He stood rigid.

''Me like a sneak and a thief,'' he murmured hoarsely, ''stealing you away! But maybe this is the end of my old life and the beginning of the new life. I'll trust my chance of it and you, if you're willing to try. Lord knows—some way may turn up! Lou, go dress! I'll wait for you at the bottom of the balcony.''

''I'll be there in one single minute—''

''Good-by, dear.''

He saw her vanish in the darkness of the room; then he swung lightly over the edge of the balcony and lowered himself, cautiously, carefully, to the ground. There he stood, looking up; for she like a white flower would lean from the vine shower above him, before long; and she, too, would climb down, and his arms would receive her! How plain it seemed to Barney that God directs all things in this world!

For a single instant a shadow crossed his mind. She was to him like an angel, with all the indescribable air of holy things about her; yet her name was Dikkon. She was of the enemy clan. And if she became his wife, the long war would have ended; he could not raise his hand against her kindred, and the blood relations of their children, if children came to them! So it would be, as he could see, the end of the old life, and the beginning of the new the instant that he received her in his arms.

Something, he thought, stirred softly behind him, and he was about to whirl, gun in hand, when an object was thrust sharply into the small of his back, and a deep voice said in a subdued tone, "Barney Quince, Barney Quince, say your prayer if you got a prayer to say, because you're dyin', Barney; you're almost dead!"

· 16 ·

IT WOULD BE FOLLY TO ATTEMPT TO MAKE ANY MOVEMENT; Quince's hand closed on a tendril of the vine and crushed the delicate leaves to nothingness.

"You're Jim Dikkon?" he said.

"I'm Jim Dikkon."

"I should've killed you the first time I met you," said Barney Quince. "I was a fool—I was a rank fool!"

"I'd give you a fair fighting chance," said Dikkon, "except that there's the girl mixed up in this. You've got to die for her sake, man!"

"I'll ask you for one thing."

"Well, ask."

"Walk me back into the trees, and finish me there."

"Ay," murmured Jim Dikkon, "because otherwise she'd know who—"

A whisper floated down from above: "Barney, Barney, darling!"

"Yes?" whispered Barney Quince. He raised his head and barely could see her.

"Are you ready for me?"

"Aye, ready!"

"I'm coming down!"

She slipped over the edge of the balcony, and Barney heard a faint murmur behind him: "Lord forgive me! Lord forgive me! She never will—"

The reaching arms of Barney received the girl and held her closely to him.

And only then she saw, and turned rigid in his arms.

"I can't do it," said Jim Dikkon suddenly. "You ought to die, Barney Quince, for her sake. But instead, if you'll go with her into the house and face her father, and tell him what you would have done with her—do you understand?"

They sat in a family circle around the fireplace, though the hearth was black and empty. Oliver Dikkon had his daughter on one side of him, and Barney Quince sat on the other.

In the background sat the captor, contributing no word to the discussion, but keeping his burning eyes fixed solemnly upon the face of the enemy of his clan.

Oliver Dikkon said at last: "I had a sort of an idea of what might come the first night that we had you here. I had an idea," he went on, leaning as though he were watching a rising flame in the fireplace, "when I saw Lou caring for you. Because there's nothing that softens the heart of a woman like seeing an enemy helpless. And Lou, here, isn't the sort that is apt to open her heart twice. Afterwards, I was pretty sure of it. All the time that you were here was a time of hell for me. I saw her growing to care about you. I couldn't send you away. I couldn't send her. She wouldn't have gone! You remember, Lou, when I wanted you to visit your aunt in Chicago?"

"I remember," she answered softly.

"Well, then the doctor came and did his work. And it seems to me that heaven has taken charge of the rest. We've hunted Barney Quince with our best men; we never could take him or hold him. Jim nearly died on the trail today. If I go to the family council and ask them, face to face, if it isn't worth while to have you for a friend, and the husband of my girl, I guess they'll rage and curse a little, but in the end they'll take you. And once you're in the clan, there'll never be a hand lifted against you by man or boy that wears the name of Dikkon. Jim, am I right?''

But Jim had stolen from the room.

Then, for the matter could not wait, Oliver Dikkon left the house to bring the family council together to decide this grave matter. Barney and Louise were left sitting, staring wide-eyed at one another.

''I begin to remember, sort of,'' said Barney Quince, suddenly closing his eyes. ''I remember a saw—a crosscut saw, Lou, that you gave me to work with—''

''Yes!''

''And the cows! And the hunting! And the woodchopping!''

''Barney, Barney, it's all coming back to you!''

''It looks to me,'' said Barney with the broadest of grins, ''as though you'd been sort of training me for the job of husband, Lou, right from the start!''